## "I've Never Done This Before,"

Hope blurted, then tensed for Murphy's reaction.

"Done what? Slept with me? I think I would've remembered." Then the full import of what she had said sank in. "Hope, are you saying…?"

She nodded miserably.

"Never?"

She shook her head.

"I'll be damned."

"Probably, and I'll still be a virgin."

Dear Reader,

Readers ask me what *I* think Silhouette Desire is. To me, Desire love stories are sexy, sassy, emotional and dynamic books about the power of love.

I demand variety, and strive to bring you six unique stories each month. These stories might be quite different, but each promises a wonderful love story with a happy ending.

This month, there's something I know you've all been waiting for: the next installment in Joan Hohl's *Big, Bad Wolfe* series, July's *Man of the Month, Wolfe Watching*. Here, undercover cop Eric Wolfe falls hard for a woman who is under suspicion.... Look for more *Big, Bad Wolfe* stories later in 1994.

As for the rest of July, well, things just keep getting hotter, starting with *Nevada Drifter,* a steamy ranch story from Jackie Merritt. And if you like your Desire books fun and sparkling, don't miss Peggy Moreland's delightful *The Baby Doctor.*

As all you "L.A. Law" fans know, there's nothing like a good courtroom drama (I *love* them myself!), so don't miss Doreen Owens Malek's powerful, gripping love story *Above the Law.* Of course, if you'd rather read about single moms trying to get single guys to love them—*and* their kids— don't miss Leslie Davis Guccione's *Major Distractions.*

To complete July we've found a tender, emotional story from a wonderful writer, Modean Moon. The book is titled *The Giving,* and it's a bit different for Silhouette Desire, so please let me know what you think about this very special love story.

So there you have it: drama, romance, humor and suspense, all rolled into six books in one fabulous line—Silhouette Desire. Don't miss any of them.

All the best,

Lucia Macro
Senior Editor

Please address questions and book requests to:
Silhouette Reader Service
U.S.: 3010 Walden Ave., P.O. Box 1325, Buffalo, NY 14269
Canadian: P.O. Box 609, Fort Erie, Ont. L2A 5X3

# DOREEN OWENS MALEK
## ABOVE THE LAW

SILHOUETTE *Desire*®
Published by Silhouette Books
America's Publisher of Contemporary Romance

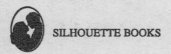

SILHOUETTE BOOKS

ISBN 0-373-05869-1

ABOVE THE LAW

Copyright © 1994 by Doreen Owens Malek

**Printed in U.S.A.**

## DOREEN OWENS MALEK

is a former attorney who decided on her current career when she sold her fledgling novel to the first editor who read it. Since then, she has gained recognition for her writing, winning honors from *Romantic Times* magazine and the coveted Golden Medallion award. She has traveled extensively throughout Europe, but it was in her home state of New Jersey that she met and married her college sweetheart. They now live in Pennsylvania.

# Prologue

---

Hope Jarvis sat in the waiting room of the mayor's office, wondering why she had been summoned to city hall. She had rescheduled her appointments for the afternoon in order to respond to the mayor's call, and the clients she had put off were on her mind.

Hope had a small solo legal practice. She was not that well-known in Philadelphia; advanced work in constitutional law and teaching an evening class at Penn Law School did not exactly bring her a lot of cases that wound up getting media coverage. But she had recently gotten a high-profile conviction and she suspected that was the reason for the telephone call from the mayor's office.

The door to the inner sanctum opened, and the mayor's secretary said, "His Honor will see you now."

Hope rose, straightening the skirt of her suit and lifting her hair off her collar. She extended her hand with a practiced smile as she strode into the lushly carpeted oak-paneled room.

"Miss Jarvis, thank you for coming," the mayor said, shaking her hand and gesturing to the empty chair placed before his desk. "Please, have a seat."

Hope sat, maintaining an expression of polite inquiry. The framed citations and plaques on the walls made the room look almost like a doctor's suite, except for the twin flags, of U.S. and Pennsylvania, standing furled in a corner of the room.

"I guess you're puzzled as to why I called you here," John Markey said. He was a short, slight man in his early fifties, with darkening blond hair and fine, aquiline features. In television interviews he always projected an aura of calm competence, and Hope felt that same air of reassuring intelligence wash over her now. Nor wonder he had been elected to what had to be one of the most difficult jobs on the planet: running a teeming northeastern city effectively while keeping its citizens satisfied that he was giving everyone a fair shake.

"Yes, I am," Hope admitted.

"I was very impressed with your handling of the Cansino case," he said.

"Thank you."

"It's not everyone who can overturn a conviction obtained by our esteemed district attorney," Markey said.

"Mr. Cansino was not properly informed of his rights. Once I was able to prove that, of course the conviction had to be vacated."

"Dennis Murphy nearly had a stroke when his verdict was reversed," the mayor said, grinning hugely.

"I'm sure one case isn't going to mar his sterling conviction rate substantially," Hope said dryly.

"Actually, that's what I wanted to discuss. There are some people who think his conviction rate is a little *too* sterling."

"Beg pardon?"

The mayor sighed and sat back in his chair. Behind him the picture window revealed the bustling span of Market Street thronged with traffic, and to his left a wilting ficus plant shed yellow leaves onto the floor. The portraits on the walls of J.F.K., Martin Luther King and the current president needed dusting; everything in city hall was showing the effects of the recent budget cuts.

"Are you aware that the district attorney's office has been coming under fire from various citizens' groups lately?"

"I've read something about it in the paper."

"Mr. Murphy has a reputation for prosecuting first and checking the fine details later."

Hope said nothing.

"While I respect his zeal to keep criminals off the streets, I have recently become concerned about the way in which some cases are being handled by the D.A.'s office. Cansino is one example. There are others. Since you are considered something of an expert in the area of First Amendment rights..."

"Oh, I don't know about that," Hope protested.

"Don't be modest. I've been talking to people around town and at the university. My information is that you have a scholarly interest in the field and that the Cansino case represents the least of what you can do. And on that note, I have a request to make of you."

Hope waited.

"I am forming a task force to investigate the D.A.'s office. I would like you to act as its head, functioning as a watchdog, if you will, overseeing the handling of criminal cases that come under its jurisdiction."

"What about my practice?" Hope asked, so surprised that she said the first thing that came into her head.

"It would be a six-month contract. I imagine that you would have to cut back on your practice or take someone on to cover you during that period."

"I assume that D.A. Murphy will not welcome my supervision," Hope said flatly. "Does he know about this yet?"

"Not yet, but if you agree I'll inform him about it."

"And if I don't agree?"

"Then I'll have to find somebody else. I am determined that this investigation take place—there's too much popular inquiry about the operation of the prosecutor's office. The Cansino case just highlighted a concern that has existed for some time." Markey picked up a pen from his blotter and began to doodle on a notepad at his elbow. "Have you ever met Dennis Murphy?"

"Once or twice briefly, at bar association functions. I've mostly seen clips of him on the news."

"He's a tough customer, but he'll be instructed to cooperate with you in every way. I wouldn't expect him to roll out the red carpet, but he's savvy enough to know that he will not be able to dodge this issue—

not when it's backed by popular momentum and my office. How do you feel about the proposition?''

"I don't know. May I have some time to think about it?''

"I'll need your decision by Friday. You'd be performing a public service if you do this, Miss Jarvis. And I'll be frank with you about something else. You have no affiliation with a political party, and that's another reason I selected you. I don't want someone going in with a preset agenda. I want a fair, impartial analysis of what's going on over there. And I'll accept your assessment. If you say there's no problem, that will be the end of it. If you point up any errors of fact or law, they will be investigated."

"I understand."

"And I don't want to underplay the magnitude of the task. You will be asked to review the handling of every criminal case where the defendant requests your assistance, and I don't have to tell you there is fertile ground for abuse there. A lot of these people will waste your time. I'll provide you with several advisory assistants, but the final judgment will be yours."

Hope nodded. "Will I be able to pick the people working with me?" she asked.

"One or two. I'd like to have representation from this office, as well."

"I see."

"How do you feel about the idea?" Markey asked again.

"A little overwhelmed."

"That's to be expected—I did spring this on you out of the blue. But as I said, I need a quick decision. And don't hesitate to call me if you have any questions."

"Thank you."

The mayor stood, and Hope did also. "I hope you will give this serious consideration," he said, shaking her hand again. "I'll expect an answer by Friday."

Hope wound up in the marble-floored hall outside his office, wondering how she had gotten there, her head spinning. It was all too much to take in at once. The proposed position was a splendid opportunity to learn and achieve a higher profile locally, and possibly do some good. But she had worked hard to build up her practice over the past five years and didn't want it to deteriorate while she was playing overseer in the D.A.'s office.

She drove home in a state of indecision, debating what to do. Since she had heard nothing about this task force before it was explained to her by Markey, the mayor had obviously decided not to reveal his plans to the media until his team was in place. The care he was taking indicated to Hope that he expected this plan to be a political hot potato.

She entered her apartment and pushed the button on her message machine, listening to the voice of her mother and then the drawl of a law school classmate who was going to be in town and wanted to get together. She called in to her office and listened to her voice mail, then dumped her handbag and her briefcase on the sofa and kicked off her shoes.

Despite the problems inherent in accepting the mayor's offer, Hope was attracted to the idea of being in the district attorney's office and observing the process there. Since passing the bar, she had always worked in a law office and never been exposed to the nitty-gritty of prosecuting on behalf of the People.

Her interest in the constitutional rights of the accused had been limited to the theoretical. While the D.A. would undoubtedly see this as a disadvantage, the mayor obviously thought she would approach the cases as a purist, and that's precisely what he wanted.

As Hope went toward the kitchen to get a drink, she passed the hall mirror, pausing to look into it as a matter of habit. Her shoulder-length dark hair was tousled from the long day and her lipstick had faded; the wide gray eyes looking back at her were tired, but intrigued with the new prospect before her.

She had decided to take the job.

# One

     —

"**Y**our Honor, did you form the task force in response to the increasing concern of the taxpayers of this city about the operation of the district attorney's office?" the reporter asked, holding his mike forward to catch Markey's answer.

"A number of factors figured into my decision," Markey answered smoothly, as Hope, sitting at his side, gazed out over the sea of faces at the press conference. She had dressed carefully for the occasion in a heathery-gray tailored suit that flattered her coloring and her tall, willowy figure. She had dealt with the media before when she handled the Cansino case, and she wanted to look as conservative and intellectual as possible in order to downplay the "Jarvis gets the job because she's a woman" angle. The mayor went on with his answer as District Attorney Murphy, looking decidedly grim at the other end of the conference table, waited for his turn at bat.

"And what about the other members of the team?" a television reporter asked as his cameraman, wearing a hat with the station's logo, panned the group from right to left.

"Attorney Jarvis has selected a former colleague of hers from the Penn Law School, Prof. Margaret Crawford, to work with her. I added two more consultants, attorneys Dansfield and McCoy, both of whom are practicing attorneys and have reputations which will ensure their impartiality."

"Will they all be on-site at the D.A.'s office every day?" the TV reporter continued.

"Attorney Jarvis will be there full-time, while the others will serve on a consulting basis."

"How does D.A. Murphy feel about all this?" another voice called loudly.

"Why don't we let him answer that for himself?" the mayor replied directly.

All eyes focused on Dennis Murphy. He was sitting with his arms folded on the table before him, leaning slightly forward into the cameras. His thick dark hair, wavy and lightly frosted with gray, was a little long, as if he didn't have time to get a haircut, but his navy suit, boiled shirt and rep tie were impeccable.

He had the broad shoulders and lean waist of an ex-football tackle who kept fit, and the joke around the city was that if Murphy didn't get you in the courtroom he might just finish the job after hours. Hope watched as he considered his words before he spoke. "I am confident," he said finally, "that the task force will be satisfied that my office, which represents the interests of the people of Philadelphia, is run properly."

"Do you regard this investigation as a vote of no confidence by the mayor?" the same reporter asked.

"I regard it as a challenge that I and my staff will be delighted to meet," Murphy answered levelly.

"Miss Jarvis, do you think you were selected for this position because of your role in the Cansino case?" a female reporter inquired, causing heads to swing in the other direction once more.

"Mayor Markey would be best equipped to answer that question," Hope replied crisply, and she saw Murphy smile slightly.

"Mr. Mayor?" the woman said.

"Miss Jarvis's experience with the Cansino appeal was only one factor in her selection," Markey answered. "She is well-grounded in the field of constitutional rights and for the last several years has run a practice devoted almost exclusively to First Amendment cases. She also has taught classes on the subject. I think it's evident that she is well qualified for the job."

"District Attorney Murphy, how will you feel about having this lovely young lady underfoot every day?" some joker in the audience called out from the back.

Murphy ignored the question until one of the reporters in the front row picked up on it and said, "Yeah, Murph, tell us."

Murphy closed his eyes and sighed audibly as Hope sank several inches in her chair.

"I expect that Miss Jarvis will behave in a professional manner and my staff will treat her the same way," he replied shortly, his face expressionless.

Hope heard very little of what happened after that. It seemed the reporters asked a few more perfunctory questions and then let them off the hook. The meeting was breaking up as Meg Crawford whispered in Hope's ear, "Did you see the look on Murphy's face? He's going to be welcoming you with a firing squad."

"Not me. *Us*."

"You're the one who'll be in his face every day. And his face isn't happy."

"I didn't expect him to be thrilled."

"Are you sure this is a good idea?" Meg asked. "It's obviously being forced on him, and it would be only natural for him to resent it."

Hope looked at her friend thoughtfully. Meg had been in her final year of law school when Hope had entered, and the older woman had been assigned as Hope's student advisor for moot court. They'd been close ever since. If this was going to be a disaster, Hope didn't want to drag Meg down in flames with her.

"If you're having second thoughts, tell me now. I can replace you on the team before this gets underway," Hope said.

"I don't want to be replaced—I want you to think about what you're doing. Murphy is powerful. He's a bad enemy to make."

Hope shrugged. "The mayor is a good friend to have and he's powerful, too."

The two women rounded a corner of the administration building and almost bumped into the subject of their conversation, who was waiting for the elevator with one of his assistant district attorneys.

Hope and Meg stopped short as Murphy caught sight of them and turned.

"Miss Jarvis," he said smoothly, "this is an opportune meeting. I was going to call you."

Hope looked up at him in silence as Meg slipped unobtrusively into the background.

"I believe we have several issues to discuss," he said. "Would you care to have lunch with me?"

His eyes were penetrating, very blue, heavily fringed by black lashes several shades darker than his hair. Hope tried to estimate his height; he topped her by four or five inches, and she was tall.

"Today, Miss Jarvis," he said, when she didn't respond.

Hope looked around for Meg, who had disappeared.

"I suppose that would be all right," she said cautiously.

Murphy looked at his assistant and said, "I'll be back in the office around two. You can reach me at Morton's if you need me."

The young man nodded and punched the button for the elevator, glancing back over his shoulder curiously.

"It'll be easier to get a cab if we go out the back way to Broad Street," Murphy said, gesturing toward the staircase.

Hope followed him down the stairs, watching his easy, graceful movements as he descended and then held the door for her at the bottom.

Hope preceded him into the spring day and stood at his side as he flagged a cab. When one glided to a stop, he held the door for Hope and then slid in next to her on the rear seat. His meticulous politeness did nothing to disguise the chill which came off him like mist from dry ice.

"Morton's on Logan Square," he said to the cabbie.

"You didn't have to take me to lunch," Hope said, to fill the silence as much as express the sentiment. "We could have met anytime for a discussion."

"Why? Do you think it'll be difficult for you to act as my watchdog after you've shared a meal with me?" he replied levelly, turning to look at her.

He had put her neatly on the defensive, and she didn't like it. "I don't regard my position on the task force in quite that way," she said stiffly.

"How do you regard it?" he asked.

"As a safeguard for defendants' rights."

"What about the victims' rights? If you had my job you'd be more impressed with the injuries done to them than the lowlifes the mayor seems to think are so important."

Hope sighed. "This debate has been raging since the Founding Fathers picked up their quills. I don't think we're going to solve it today. It seems that we're stuck with each other, so why don't we make the best of it?"

Murphy stared out the window and offered no reply, his mouth a tight line. When they reached the restaurant, he paid the cabbie and opened the door for Hope without looking at her.

"Mr. D.A., how are you doing today?" the maître d' said to Murphy, coming forward to shake his hand. "I didn't know you would be joining us for lunch."

"I didn't know it, either, Buddy. I don't have a reservation. What can you do for me?"

"I'm sure we can find a nice table for you and the lovely young lady," Buddy said with a wide smile, obviously thinking that Hope was Murphy's date.

"A quiet table, Buddy—this is a working lunch," Murphy said briskly, correcting Buddy's mistaken impression neatly.

"Right-o," Buddy said slowly, looking from one to the other inquiringly before disappearing inside the bustling main room. Murphy and Hope waited tensely for him to return, and when he did he led them to an upstairs table at the back where the din from the crowded first floor was barely audible.

"This is great, Buddy. Thanks," Murphy said, and slipped Buddy a tip as he held out a chair for Hope.

"Your waiter is Bill and he'll be right over to explain our offerings," Buddy said.

"Get whatever you like, it's not on the city's tab," Murphy said shortly.

"Doesn't this qualify for your expense account?" Hope inquired icily, taking her cue from him. "After all, neither of us would consider it a personal encounter, since we certainly wouldn't be here if it weren't job-related."

He looked up at her, and Hope was surprised to see that there was a trace of a smile on his lips. "You haven't changed at all," he said quietly, in a tone that made her breath catch in her throat.

"What do you mean?" she asked warily.

"We've met before—don't you remember?"

"I recall seeing you at bar association meetings...." she answered vaguely.

He shook his head. "I was one of the judges at your moot-court competition, the end of your first year," he said. "I was in private practice then."

Hope stared at him. She had been such a nervous wreck that day, trying to remember all her arguments and get her points across, that Genghis Khan could have been sitting on the panel and she wouldn't have noticed.

"You shook my hand and thanked me nicely afterward for awarding you the victory. Obviously I made a tremendous impression," he said dryly.

"I'm sorry," Hope replied, flustered. "That whole experience is a blur. I was so convinced I was going to blow it, that when I survived, everything else just sort of merged into a sublime ocean of relief."

"You did more than survive—you won hands down," Murphy said. "I have a vivid recollection of your rapier directness. It's what came to mind when I was informed that you were to take on this glorious mission for our esteemed mayor."

The waiter arrived, saving Hope from a reply. He was wheeling a cart on which various cuts of beef and other entrées were displayed uncooked on plates, ready for selection. He started to recite the litany of available items, describing each in vivid detail, but Hope cut him short.

"I think I'll just have a Cobb salad and an iced tea," she said, looking away from the bounty of raw food.

"I'll have the eight-ounce sirloin, rare, and a house salad with vinaigrette dressing," Murphy said. "You can take the rest of that away, please."

Bill rolled the trolley down the aisle toward the kitchen and left them alone.

"I wondered why we didn't receive menus," Hope said breathlessly.

"You aren't the first person to find that display vulgar," Murphy replied dismissively.

Their eyes met across the table.

"Shall we get down to it?" he said pointedly.

"By all means," Hope responded crisply.

"I don't want your investigation to disrupt the operation of my office," he said bluntly.

"It won't."

"I don't want you combing through my files looking for an ax to grind," he continued.

"You know that's not how the task force is designed to operate. I will examine only those cases the defendant, or the defendant's attorney, brings to my attention."

"Which will be all of them," Murphy said with disgust.

"Don't be ridiculous."

He sighed and sat back in his chair, staring at her. "Miss Jarvis, you have been operating out of your ivory tower too long. We had a press conference this morning. By this afternoon, every cheap pimp, burglar, rapist and repeat felon in Philadelphia is going to be lining up with a list of grievances for you to examine on Monday."

"Don't you think you're exaggerating just a bit?"

He smiled thinly. "You'll see."

Bill brought their lunches.

"That was fast," Hope said.

"You don't have to sound so grateful," Murphy commented. "Are you timing this conference?"

"Is that what this is? It feels somewhat like an interview with the KGB."

"May I continue?" he asked archly.

"Please do."

"I don't want your presence in my office to intimidate my people in the performance of their duties," he went on doggedly, digging into his salad.

"I think it will be your job to keep them on track," Hope replied, picking up her fork.

"So you're not going to admit that your presence could have a chilling effect?" he asked.

"It's not designed to do that."

"Come on, most of my assistant district attorneys are kids just out of law school. They're not going to want to make a mistake, do something that will get them into trouble with city hall. They'll be tiptoeing around these crooks, afraid to proceed against them because you might find fault with what they're doing."

"From what I've observed, I *should* find fault with some of the things that go on in your office."

He shot her a look that would have frozen an active volcano. "Are we talking about Cansino?" he said.

"That's just one example."

Murphy clenched his fist on the table. "Cansino is a career criminal who deserves to spend several lifetimes behind bars," he said through his teeth.

"That does not alter the fact that the policeman did not recite the complete Miranda warning of his rights when he arrested him."

"By the time that incident took place, Cansino had been arrested so many times he could have recited the Miranda warning himself—in his sleep!" Murphy replied, in a tone of barely suppressed rage.

"So he was not entitled to constitutional protection, because you felt his yellow sheet was too long?" Hope asked sweetly.

It was several seconds before he said, with forced calm, "I can see that we're going to get along beautifully."

Bill arrived with Murphy's steak. Hope watched as he speared it with his fork and cut off a small piece.

"You bleeding-heart liberals make me sick," he said, staring at her, a pulse beating at his temple.

"Now we get down to it," Hope replied.

"You should all be forced to spend the night in the prearraignment tank with some of these charmers you're trying so desperately to spring," he added tersely, chewing.

"You're not going to win this argument with me— I've heard it all before. Everyone is entitled to the protection of the law. Even those you think don't deserve it."

He sighed heavily and put down his fork, studying her across the table. "Aren't you going to eat?" he asked. "You haven't touched your salad."

"I'm not very hungry," she said truthfully.

"I guess you think I brought you here today to give you a hard time," he said.

"Did you?" she countered.

"No. I just didn't want you to start on Monday with any misconceptions. Once you report for work, I won't have the time to say these things to you."

"Then thank you so much. I wouldn't have wanted to miss out on this experience," Hope said dryly.

They finished the meal in strained silence, and when Bill returned to ask if they wanted dessert, Murphy paid him and left the tip. Hope took a last sip of her ice tea and stood briskly.

"If there's nothing else . . . ?" she said.

"What, are you leaving?" Murphy asked, glancing over her shoulder as if looking for somebody she might be joining.

"Is there some reason I shouldn't?"

He stood and shoved back his chair. "I'll see you outside and get you a cab," he said brusquely.

"That won't be necessary," Hope replied, but he ignored her, waiting until she walked forward and then falling into step behind her. No matter how rude she might find his personal opinions, it was clear that his idea of proper etiquette would be observed.

On the sidewalk a fresh breeze was enlivening the early afternoon as Murphy gestured to a cab waiting in line at the curb. As it glided toward them, he said, "Are you going home or back to your office?"

"Home," she replied.

"Take the lady to 1822 Walnut Street," he said to the cabbie, leaning in the passenger window and handing the man a bill. Then he opened the back door and took Hope's hand to help her into the cab. As she stepped forward, her heel caught in a crack on the sidewalk and she tumbled backward into his arms.

It all happened so fast that afterward she had difficulty recalling the exact sequence of events that left her clinging to him as he set her back on her feet. But there were other impressions that she later wished she *could* dismiss: the strength of his grip as he lifted her, the feel of his muscular body pressed against hers, the clean soap and starch and pressed-wool smell of him. They were close for only a few seconds, but for Hope it was a moment frozen in time.

She was so flustered when he released her that she could not meet his eyes.

"Are you all right?" he asked, looming over her as the cabbie waited, watching the two of them over his shoulder.

"Of course, I just turned my ankle, so stupid of me," she babbled, almost lunging into the cab in her effort to get free of him. She could feel that her face was flaming.

"Are you sure?" he said, lingering on the curb.

"Fine, fine. Goodbye." She nodded to the cabbie to take off as Murphy stood gazing after her, his face in the rearview mirror wearing an inscrutable expression.

It was only after she had traveled several blocks that she wondered something else.

Why had Murphy known her home address?

# TWO

___

"So was it a dead loss, or what?" Meg asked, curled on Hope's sofa, holding a cup of tea. It was the following afternoon, and both women were relaxing after a workout at their gym.

"We didn't exactly get along like a house on fire," Hope replied, sitting next to her. Spring rain was darkening the day and a small blaze crackled in Hope's living room fireplace.

"Did you have a fight?"

"Not quite. He just conveyed the impression that my concerns were inexpressibly stupid, and I let him know I thought he was the prime persecutor of the underclass in Philadelphia."

"Sounds like you had a jolly time. I wonder why he wanted to take you out at all."

"He was trying to intimidate me. One-on-one works better than glaring at me across a room, which you may recall he tried at the press conference."

Meg sighed. "You have to admit he's cute."

"Hmph."

"What is that supposed to mean?"

"It means I can't let something superficial like that interfere with my job."

"Oh. I understand. You've been struck blind."

"Don't be offensive Meg. Anyway, he's married."

"Nope."

"What? He's not married?"

"Aha. Look how interested she is."

"I'm not interested. I just remembered hearing that he got married while we were both away—you in Boston and me in Harrisburg. It was several years ago."

"His wife died, some accident or something, I don't know the details. It was pretty awful—if I remember right, she was pregnant at the time she died."

"Oh, no."

"Yeah. It helps a little to understand that hard shell of his, doesn't it?"

Hope said nothing, merely stared into the fire pensively.

"He got to you, didn't he?" Meg said softly.

Hope shook her head.

"Then what is it?"

"I'm wondering how I can operate this task force right under his nose when he's so dead against it. I'm sure he makes a formidable opponent."

"He'd make a formidable anything. He's the youngest district attorney in the city's history."

Hope turned back to her friend curiously. "What else do you know about him?"

"This inquiry is purely professional, right?"

"Right. Know your enemy—it's the first rule of combat according to the Marine Corps manual."

"If you ever read the newspapers you'd have the same information I do."

"It's all bad news. I'd usually rather listen to music."

"Let me see," Meg said, scanning the ceiling as if Murphy's history were written there. "He comes from South Philly, poor family, went to college on a football scholarship. Then law school on some work-study thing, private practice until his wife died. Then he was working in the D.A.'s office, and shortly after he became the D.A. What they call a meteoric rise. I'm not clear on a lot of the details, except that since he's been running to the prosecutor's office, conviction rates have soared and all the city liberals have been screaming bloody murder."

"A real hard guy, that's what they say," Hope observed quietly, running the tip of her finger around the rim of her cup.

"Did you see something to counter that impression?"

Hope shrugged. "Oh, he sounded tough, all right, but there's a look in his eye . . ."

"What look?"

Hope gestured dismissively. "Don't listen to me—I don't know what I'm saying."

"You'd better be careful, Hope. This assignment may not be the career boon you're hoping for if you run afoul of this guy and he makes life miserable for you."

Hope nodded and got up, carrying her cup to the kitchen and setting it in the sink.

"So tomorrow's the beginning," Meg observed. "I'm glad I'll just be serving in an advisory capacity and don't have to show up there every day."

"You're inspiring me with so much confidence, Meg."

"Thrilled to hear it. And on that note, I'd better get home. Exams are in ten days and my first-year law students are getting very twitchy. I promised them a course review this week and I have to prepare it."

"Good luck," Hope said, as Meg shrugged into her rain slicker and zipped it up.

"I'll need it. I hardly remember the stuff myself at this point." Meg waved as she drew the hood over her head. She only lived a couple of blocks away and was going to walk.

After Meg left, Hope tidied the apartment, folding up magazines, loading the dishwasher and dumping take-out containers into the trash. She made her Sunday duty call to her mother and left a message for Greg Collins, the colleague who was temporarily taking over the cases from her practice. Then she sat on the chintz-covered sofa in front of her picture window and stared out at the falling rain.

The coming morning would bring a big change to her life, but she was ready for it. She was bored with her perfectly decorated twelfth-floor apartment, complete with fireplace, trash compactor and Jacuzzi tub. Bored with her lunches with friends, and bored with als who professed their belief in women's equality but really wanted to take her to bed as quickly as possible.

She had been engaged during law school to a very nice man who was stunned by her refusal to marry him as soon as they graduated. Hope was unable to explain it herself, except that she couldn't imagine having sex with him for the rest of her life. In fact, she couldn't imagine having sex with him at all. She broke it off when he pressed her to sleep with him. He later married a nurse from Johnstown, and they now had two kids.

Hope wished Todd well but never regretted her decision. And if it weren't for her mother nagging her about the lack of grandchildren and the opportunity for bliss in the suburbs that Hope had thrown away, she wouldn't even think about it.

Hope rose and went into the bedroom to pick out an outfit for the next day.

"And this will be your office. We've cleared it out as best we could, but I'm afraid there isn't much space," Sue Chancellor informed Hope apologetically. She was the assistant district attorney assigned as Hope's liaison and was showing her around the complex in city hall.

"This will be fine," Hope said, setting her briefcase on the scarred desk. The room was about nine-by-twelve with shelves on three sides and a frosted glass door leading to the hall. Dusty piles of manila folders from the previous occupant remained stacked on a table against the far wall.

"Here's your terminal. I assume you're IBM compatible," Sue said, gesturing to the monitor sitting on the desk.

Hope nodded.

"All the police blotter information comes right through there. Any case you want to look up, just type in the references and you'll get everything you need to know, right down to the arresting officers and the perpetrator's previous record."

"Thank you, that's very convenient."

Sue, a petite blonde with a boyish haircut and double earring studs in both ears, pointed to a stack of slips next to the computer.

"I'm afraid you already have a bunch of cases to look over, requested by defendants or their attorneys," she said. "There's enough in that pile to keep you busy for the morning. Just bring me the ones you want to pursue further and I'll pass them on to Murphy's office. Coffee is by the watercooler, and I'm right down the hall if you need me."

"Thanks, Sue. You've been a big help."

Sue grinned and saluted. "Welcome to the third level of the inferno—liars and cheaters."

Hope smiled back. "Is that where I am?"

"Sure. Didn't you see the sign over the main entrance? 'All hope abandon, you who enter here.'"

Hope chuckled as Sue disappeared from the doorway. Then she took off her jacket, picked up the stack of case referrals and turned on the computer.

Two hours later, Hope had to admit that from what she could see so far, Murphy had been right. The complaints she'd been examining had about as much merit as the horde of ne'er-do-wells asserting they'd been promised legacies by Howard Hughes. As the clock on the wall scrolled past eleven, she got up and headed for the ladies' room, taking a minute to brush her hair and refresh her lipstick. She stopped at the coffee urn on the way back and as she turned with the cup in her hand she encountered Dennis Murphy.

He was wearing a charcoal-gray suit of a very subtle glen plaid, with a figured gray tie that made his vivid eyes take on the brackish hue of still water. He surveyed her unsmilingly and said, "Are you all settled in?"

"Yes, thank you. I'm very comfortable."

"Just let Sue know if you need anything," he added, and walked away. Hope stood looking after him, noting that he had not volunteered to intervene personally in her business.

Evidently, he had assigned Sue the express mission of keeping Hope off his back.

The ensuing days followed pretty much the same pattern. Hope arrived in the morning, sifted through a pile of baseless claims, had lunch, and then repeated the same procedure in the afternoon. Murphy favoured her with a frosty nod when he encountered her in the halls, but otherwise she didn't see him. The job was turning out to be something she hadn't expected—dull—when after about two weeks she finally came across a case that required further inquiry. Hope requested a conference with Mr. Murphy.

She was duly ushered into the august presence of the district attorney late one Friday afternoon. Hope looked around at the lacquered walls of his office, the framed degrees hanging at precise angles, the single spider plant on a table by the window. The room was clean and correct, but characterless. It bore no trace of the personality of the man sitting behind the desk.

"Sue tells me you have a question about the Landau case," Murphy said, looking up from a yellow legal pad where he was making notes. His blinding white shirt and striped tie made him look like an advertisment for blue-chip stocks.

"That's right."

He produced a manila file from several piles on his desk. "What is it?"

"The police searched the Landau apartment when they arrested Mr. Landau," Hope said, setting her briefcase on the floor. She was ready to go home and resented being put off until the man was practically out the door for the weekend.

"So? He gave his consent."

"He was dead drunk at the time," Hope said flatly, locking her gaze with his.

Murphy eyed her levelly across the distance that separated them. "What makes you say that, Miss Jarvis?" he asked in a tone of exaggerated patience.

"He had a blood alcohol level of 0.2. That's legally drunk in this jurisdiction. He was incapable of giving informed consent for the police to search his home. The officers should have taken him into custody and then obtained a search warrant, or waited until he sobered up and then asked him to grant permission."

"Miss Jarvis, there is a time factor in these cases. The police were looking for fresh evidence and they found it. If they had waited, as you suggest, an accomplice could have removed the drugs from the apartment or any number of things could have happened."

"That does not negate the fact that the police conducted an illegal search."

"I assume Landau is now complaining about this?"

"His lawyer is. His case was presented for my review."

"What are you going to do?"

"My job. I'm referring this one to the mayor." She stood briskly and turned toward the door.

"You do realize that Landau is a career criminal?" Murphy asked her belligerently.

"The law should be applied equally to everyone, regardless of history. I believe you should have encountered that principle in Con Law 101, first year."

"Don't lecture me, Miss Jarvis. If you had my job—"

"If I had your job I wouldn't want my police force to conduct illegal searches," she said, reaching for the doorknob.

Murphy was out of his seat and blocking her path before she could step aside.

"Congratulations, Miss Jarvis. Thomas Jefferson would be proud of you. You've upheld his highest ideals with your campaign to get this piece of scum out of jail."

"It's not a campaign, Mr. Murphy. It's merely a referral for further consideration—exactly what I was sent here to do. Would you please let me pass?"

They were glaring at one another when a knock sounded on the door from the other side.

"Murph?" a female voice said. "It's Sue—we're leaving now. Are you ready to go?"

Murphy's expression indicated he had no idea what Sue was talking about, and didn't care. He yanked open the door.

"Go where?" he said testily.

"For drinks at Hopalong's," Sue replied, glancing from Murphy to Hope and then back again. "Everybody's waiting. We're celebrating my passing the New York bar. Don't you remember?"

Murphy obviously didn't.

"I forgot you were in here, Hope. I'm sorry. Why don't you come with us?" Sue added pleasantly.

"Oh no," Hope demurred.

At the same time, Murphy said, "I'm going to be some time here—why don't you go without me?"

"I won't hear of it," Sue said firmly to Murphy. "You work much too hard, and, anyway, you promised. You know how much I studied for that test, I demand some recognition. And Hope, you've hardly met anyone else in this office. You're always surgically attached to that computer. It's Friday. Why don't you join us and relax for a while?"

Murphy and Hope both stared at her, stymied.

A group of several assistants formed behind Sue, grinning expectantly at their boss.

"Come on, Murph, you said you'd pick up the tab," one of them called cheerfully. "You can't back out now."

Murphy sighed, accepting defeat, and ushered them all into the main hall, locking the door of his office behind them. Hope had taken several steps toward the front door when Sue seized her arm.

"Oh no, you don't. You can spare twenty minutes for a drink—I don't care how hot your date is."

"No date," Hope said ruefully.

"Then maybe we can find you one. Happy hour at Hopalong's is *very* congenial."

What Hope really wanted was a hot bath and escape from Murphy's flinty stare, but Sue had a death grip on her arm. Hope allowed herself to be steered out the double front doors of the Justice Building, mingling with the chattering group of Murphy's subordinates. They walked down the block and around the corner to the neighborhood bar, which was congested and smoky and already roaring with the end-of-the-week "thank God it's Friday" crowd. But even over the din, Hope could hear Murphy's deep voice, floating like a leitmotiv in the mix of sounds. As they settled at the curving bar, Hope was aware of him to her left, talking to an assistant named David Clendon.

"So, how's the job going?" Sue asked, settling onto a stool next to Hope. "Finding any gross misconduct in our esteemed office?"

"Not much," Hope admitted.

"What'll you have, ladies?" the bartender asked, appearing in front of them.

"Margarita," Sue said. "And make sure to hand the bill directly to that handsome gentleman over there," she added wickedly, gesturing airily at Murphy.

"Will do." The bartender looked expectantly at Hope, rubbing the counter with a rag.

"Perrier with a twist," she said.

Sue made a face. "Give her a margarita, too," she said, tapping her foot to the beat of the band in the background.

"Oh, no, please. I don't like them," Hope said.

The bartender waited.

"Dubonnet red," Hope conceded.

"My grandmother drinks Dubonnet," Sue said darkly, biting into a pretzel as the bartender vanished.

"I'm sorry I'm so dull," Hope replied, smiling.

"I don't know—for a dull person you shook up our office pretty good when your mission was announced," Sue said archly.

"Really?"

"*He* was not at all pleased," Sue said, nodding in Murphy's direction.

"That I know."

"Me, I was glad to see you arrive. The D.A.'s office wields a lot of unchecked power—it won't hurt us to undergo a little scrutiny." She accepted her drink from the bartender and added soberly, "Though I would never say so to you-know-who."

Hope nodded as the bartender handed her the small glass of sherry she had ordered.

"To the loyal opposition," Sue said, raising her glass to Hope dramatically.

Hope returned the gesture and took a sip.

"I felt a little funny coming here with you, considering what my job is," Hope confessed.

Sue made a dismissive gesture. "Don't worry about it—nobody takes it personally except Murphy. He regards the office as an extension of his own integrity."

*Great,* Hope thought. "So you passed the New York bar?" she said brightly, seeking to change the subject.

Sue nodded, taking another sip of her drink. "I'm moving there in the fall—thought I'd get a head start on it. It's a toughie, and Murphy bet me I wouldn't pass on the first try. That's what this little event is celebrating—his defeat." She giggled.

"I guess he doesn't suffer many," Hope volunteered.

Sue nodded agreement. "Look at him," she said wistfully. "I've been trying to get him to see me as something other than a colleague for three years. No dice."

Hope followed the direction of Sue's gaze. Murphy's tie was pulled loose from its knot and he was deeply involved in conversation with David, a half-filled glass of dark liquid in his hand.

"When he looks at me he sees 'lawyer' and 'work-horse' tattooed on my forehead. 'Woman' does not seem to be on the menu."

Hope glanced back at Sue, her streaked blond hair, even features and slender figure. It would be difficult not to notice her feminine attributes.

"Yes, I know. I can't figure it, either," Sue said dispiritedly. "He's not gay, but he's not interested. Woe is me." She finished her drink and stood. "I'm going to hit the ladies' room. Want to come along?"

Hope looked at the crush of people between their location and the rest rooms and shook her head.

"Be right back," Sue said, and she began to thread her way through the throng.

Hope played with her untouched drink for a couple of minutes and then decided that she had stayed long enough to be polite. She was about to tap Clara Miller, another assistant district attorney, and ask her to make apologies to Sue, when Sue's empty seat was taken abruptly by a large and clearly inebriated man in a gray sweat suit.

"How ya doin'?" he said to Hope, leaning in close enough to give her a strong blast of his incendiary breath.

Hope nodded glacially and began to detach herself unobtrusively from her seat.

"Where ya goin'?" he said querulously, dropping a massive paw on her arm.

"I'm late for an appointment," Hope lied, glancing around desperately for the bouncer, who was nowhere to be seen.

Her admirer's huge fingers closed around her wrist. "You wouldn't be just tryin' to get away from me, now, would ya?" he muttered menacingly.

Hope craned her neck for Sue, but the crowd was a sea of nameless faces and the door to the rest room remained closed. She tried catch the bartender's eye, but he was taking a long order and didn't look her way.

"What's the harm in havin' a little drink with me?" the large man said, tightening his grip as Hope resisted.

Suddenly an arm was draped across Hope's shoulders and Murphy kissed her cheek soundly.

"Hi, honey. Sorry to keep you waiting," he said, deftly extricating her from the behemoth's grasp. "We'd better get going—we're late." He smiled engagingly at Hope's stunned tormentor and said, "Hi, there. How's it going?"

"What kept you?" Hope said, taking her cue and stepping quickly behind Murphy. "It seems like I've been waiting for hours."

"Oh, the traffic, you know. Friday is hell."

"You shouldn't leave her alone in a place like this," the man said drunkenly to Murphy, recovering slowly. "Lots of guys around with only one thing on their minds."

"You're absolutely right, and thanks for looking out for her," Murphy replied, taking Hope's arm in proprietary fashion and leading her toward the door. "Have a good weekend," he called over his shoulder to the drunk as they left.

Hope maintained a dignified silence until they were out on the sidewalk with the spring dusk gathering around them.

"Thank you," she finally said grudgingly.

"You're welcome. I could see from across the room that you were in trouble."

"I can get home from here," Hope announced, eager to get away. She didn't like feeling indebted to him.

"How?"

"Crosstown bus—my car is in the shop. The stop is just on that corner," she said, pointing.

"On a Friday evening? You'll wait there forever, probably get accosted by another drunk stumbling out of the bar. My car is in the lot down the street. I got to the office late and the parking garage was full today. I'll take you home."

Hope hesitated.

"I'll flag a cab for you if you'd prefer not to ride in my car," he said stiffly.

He was making her feel ridiculous, which, of course, was his intention.

"All right," Hope agreed.

They walked down the block together, Hope acutely conscious of the tall man at her side. She hurried to match her stride to his long one. He presented his ticket to the valet and then waited, arms folded, as Hope looked everywhere but at him.

"Relax," he finally said. "Remember me? I'm the guy who just saved you."

Hope managed a weak smile as his car, a sleek black foreign sedan, glided to a stop next to them. He tipped the valet and then held the passenger door open for Hope, waiting until she arranged her briefcase on the floor before closing the door. When he slid in next to her, the scent she had noticed before—all soap and starch and rampant masculinity—seemed to fill the car. She stared deliberately out the window. Why was she always so conscious of him?

He drove directly to her building in silence, without asking directions, and then said as he braked to a stop, "My car phone isn't working. I have to check in with booking down at the station. Do you mind if I use your phone?"

When Hope didn't answer immediately, he said neutrally, "If it's an imposition, I can always stop at a pay phone."

Why did he always make her feel like the killjoy spinster aunt at a teenage keg party? "Of course it's not an imposition. You can leave the car with the doorman and come on up."

There was another strained silence as they ascended in the elevator to her apartment. She unlocked the door as he stood behind her and then he followed her inside.

"Very nice," he said, looking around him.

"Thank you." It was strange to have him invading her space. He seemed to overwhelm the daintily appointed rooms like a rugby player at a baby shower.

"The phone is right over there," Hope said, indicating the counter which separated the kitchen from the dining area.

He nodded. Taking off his jacket and draping it over his arm, he punched out a number on the phone and then said into the receiver, "It's Murphy. What's going on?"

He listened for a long moment and then said, "Call me back. I'm at..." He recited Hope's number, reading off the dial, and then replaced the receiver in its cradle.

"Can I get you a drink while you wait?" Hope said politely. "Coffee—something stronger?"

"Coffee's fine," he replied shortly, removing a small notebook from the breast pocket of his shirt. He scribbled something in it and then looked up at Hope.

"I'm sorry about the delay, but I need this information right away. Is it okay for me to wait?"

"Perfectly fine," Hope replied, as she placed a filter in the coffee machine and then filled the jug with water.

"Have you been reading in the papers about the Sanders murder?" Murphy asked.

"I saw it on the news this morning."

"We made an arrest late last night and the suspect was arraigned today. I want to know if he's going to make bail."

"Is it likely he will?"

Murphy shrugged. "You'd be amazed how some of these people can come up with money."

Hope plugged in the coffee machine and flicked the switch. "Do you regard him as dangerous?"

Murphy favored her with a jaded smile. "I regard them all as dangerous. I guess that's the difference between you and me."

"I regard them as dangerous," Hope replied primly. "I just feel they should be accorded their civil rights."

"Very admirable," Murphy said sarcastically.

The telephone rang shrilly. He reached over immediately and grabbed the receiver.

"Murphy," he barked. He listened and then said, "Thanks. I'll be right there." He hung up and shrugged into his jacket.

"What happened?" Hope asked.

"He's out. I guess some little do-gooder like yourself coughed up his bail."

Hope let that pass and said, "Coffee's ready. I have some paper cups—you can take it with you."

He straightened his tie. "Thanks," he said grudgingly.

Hope poured the coffee as he walked over to stand next to her, watching her hands at work.

"Cream?" she asked.

"Black," he replied.

Hope turned to hand him the cup and splashed the hot liquid all over her arm. The cup went flying to the floor in a flood of coffee as she gasped in pain.

Murphy turned on the cold tap in the sink full force and thrust her arm under the gush of water. "Just hold it there," he said, and yanked open the freezer door, decanting several ice cubes. Hope sighed with relief as he rubbed them on her scorched skin.

"I don't know why I'm so clumsy," she said, when she could speak again. But she did know. His nearness had made her nervous.

"Could happen to anybody," he observed.

"It usually happens to me," she replied, as she gazed in dismay at the mess on the floor.

"Have you got any ointment?" he asked.

"In the bathroom. The first-aid kit is on the second shelf of the linen closet behind the door."

He went into the bathroom and returned with a square box with a red cross on its top. Working methodically, he smeared the burn with the soothing salve.

"I could do this myself," Hope said, embarrassed at her apparent helplessness.

"Not as well as I can," he replied shortly. "I have two hands." He wrapped the burned spot in gauze and taped the dressing in place efficiently.

"Thank you," Hope said, looking up at him.

"You're welcome," he murmured, holding her gaze.

The telephone rang again.

"Damn," Murphy muttered under his breath, releasing her to answer it. "Just a second, please." He looked over at Hope. "I thought it would be the precinct again," he said, "but it's your mother."

Hope groaned inwardly. She knew she would have quite a time explaining the presence of this man in her apartment to the long arm of Long Island.

"Please tell her I'll call her back in a few minutes," Hope said, aware that putting off the conversation indefinitely was not going to avoid it.

He did so and hung up the phone. "I have to go," he said. "Will you be all right?"

"Fine."

"Are you sure?"

"Absolutely."

He headed for the door. "Good night," he said, turning back to face her.

"Good night. Thanks for the lift home. And for the first aid—it was kind of you to help."

He nodded and was gone in two seconds, leaving a void in her apartment, as if he had taken the furniture with him.

Hope spent about ten minutes cleaning up the coffee spill and thinking over what had just transpired, and then went reluctantly back to the phone. "Hello, Mother," she said resignedly when Mrs. Jarvis answered.

"Who was that who answered the phone?" Mrs. Jarvis demanded, not bothering with any preliminaries.

"That was the Philadelphia district attorney, Mother."

"What was he doing in your apartment?"

"I work with him now. He brought me home."

"I thought you were supposed to be overseeing the activities of his office."

"That's right."

"Then you're his adversary. Why is he being so chummy?"

"He's not being chummy, Mother—he just did me a favor. Do you have to make a federal case out of it?"

"How old is he?"

Hope looked at the ceiling. "I haven't seen his social security file, Mother. I don't know. Why don't you try the FBI?"

"Well, how old does he *look?*" her mother demanded, ignoring the sarcasm.

"About thirty-five, I guess."

"That's young for a district attorney, especially of a big city, isn't it?"

"Yes."

"Is he married?"

"I think he was, but I heard his wife died. Enough of the interrogation, Mother. If you ever decide to quit teaching kindergarten, you could use your skills when questioning spies."

"Forget the smart remarks, young lady. I don't want you getting involved with your boss. You and I both know what a nightmare that can be."

"Mother, I broke up with Todd because I didn't want to marry him, not because he was my supervisor at the law firm where we worked when we were in school. And Dennis Murphy is not my boss. My assignment is temporary and I report directly to the mayor."

"Murphy? He's Irish?"

"I guess so, Mother. Most people named Murphy are."

"Does he drink?"

"Mother, I am not going to have this conversation. If you don't change the subject right now, I am hanging up."

Hope's doorbell rang.

"I have to go, Mother, there's someone at the door."

"Don't put me off with that excuse."

"There is genuinely someone at the door, Mother. Goodbye." Hope hung up, shaking her head in exasperation, and walked over to her foyer to open the door.

"Hope Jarvis?" the delivery man said.

"Yes, but I didn't order anything."

"Fletcher's Pharmacy." He handed her a package, saluted and went off down the hall.

Hope opened the bag and found a note inside, along with a tube of antibiotic cream.

*"My brother is a doctor,"* the note said. *"I had him call in this prescription for you. Take care of that arm."*

It was signed *"D. Murphy."*

# Three

---

When Hope returned to the D.A.'s office on Monday, it was as if the incident the previous Friday had never happened. Murphy maintained his usual distance, asking once about her burn. When she replied that it was fine, he dropped the subject completely. Hope was at first puzzled, then disappointed, and finally as the days passed with no further comment from him, resigned. Had she imagined the intimacy between them, the look on his face as he ministered to her injury? What had prompted his thoughtfulness in sending along the salve if he now displayed nothing but indifference?

Hope tried to dismiss his attitude, which became easier when her referral on the Landau case got no further than the mayor's desk, and she consequently had nothing to say to Murphy. Hope worked alone at her computer and rarely saw him, as he was busy with his new murder case and the thousands of other cases that were already pending.

Weeks passed as they nodded at each other in the halls, and Hope grew increasingly perturbed by her lack of progress in turning up questionable cases. Maybe Murphy *was* right, and there was nothing to find.

"Do you know anything about the Kirk burglary?" Hope asked Sue Chancellor one day when Sue was in her office, collecting money for lunch orders.

"Kirk?" Sue said. "The name doesn't ring a bell. What are the facts?"

"Felon named Robert Kirk was ransacking a condo when the owner came home and caught him in the act. Kirk attacked the owner and put her in the hospital. He was charged with first-degree burglary and assault, pled down to third-degree. He's now doing two to five in Graterford."

"Sounds just like a lot of them we get around here," Sue replied, shrugging. "What's different about it?"

"Kirk's P.D. requested that I take a look at his case—it's on appeal. And I have to tell you, I think there's a real problem."

Sue glanced over her shoulder and then shut the door to the hall. "No use getting Dennis all twitchy if this comes to nothing," she said quietly.

"Well, the mayor didn't think the Landau case was worth pursuing, but I know he'll want to follow up on this."

"Why?"

"Mr. Kirk is already serving his sentence, and he should never have been convicted."

Sue eyed her warily.

"The home owner pulled a gun on Mr. Kirk when she found him robbing her house. The force he used was self-defense, and it was lesser force than she had at her command. He was not armed."

"But he was burglarizing her property!" Sue said.

"That doesn't matter—he was allowed to defend himself. You know the law as well as I do, Sue. The jury confused the issues of burglary and assault, and the judge let them do it."

"Dennis is going to pull another Landau number when he hears this," Sue said in a warning tone.

Hope shrugged.

"Let me pull this guy's yellow sheet before we say anything to Murphy," Sue added, opening the door to the hall. She returned minutes later with a computer printout, her expression bleak.

"Bad news?" Hope asked.

"The worst." Sue looked down at the paper she held. "Felonies dating back fifteen years to juvy, assorted crimes of violence and property damage, car theft, et cetera." She paused and looked up at Hope. "Two counts of rape dismissed when the complainants dropped the charges."

"Two different women?" Hope said.

Sue nodded.

"Which means their lawyers convinced them they wouldn't be up to the ordeal of proving a charge of rape in court."

"Probably."

"Which also means that Kirk could have raped them."

Sue looked even gloomier. "Right again."

Kirk's record was a lot worse than Landau's, and Hope would be lobbying to put Kirk back on the street. Sue was right, Hope thought. Murphy would go ballistic.

"Do you want me to tell Dennis?" Sue asked.

"No, that's my job. Just ask if he will see me as soon as possible today."

"Okay." Sue left, and about ten minutes later the telephone in Hope's office rang.

"Hello?" Hope said, distracted, still reading Kirk's file.

"It's Murphy."

Hope put the file aside and waited.

"Sue tells me you have another candidate for rehabilitation," Murphy said dryly.

"I have a candidate for release. The man should not be incarcerated at all."

Murphy sighed. "I know this guy Kirk. He's not Landau or even Cansino. They were small-time cruds, cruising on the edge, involved with all petty stuff. Kirk's a real bad actor, a sociopath. I'd advise you to forget it."

"I can't. His public defender asked me to review his case, and he never should have been charged with assault. He's already done enough time to cover the burglary. He should be out."

There was a long pause at Murphy's end of the line. Then, "Look, do you have a few minutes after work to talk about this? We could grab a bite at Bookbinder's and see if we can reach an agreement."

Hope hesitated, wondering what tactic Murphy was employing. Did he think that sweet reason and a little wining and dining might accomplish what his usual blind fury never could? Hope was not deceived that his intentions had changed. He was merely trying to persuade her by different methods.

"I don't know. . . ." she said, waffling.

"Do you have something else planned?"

"No."

"Then why not? We both have to eat."

"All right," Hope said, thinking that she seemed to be spending a lot of time in restaurants with this man she hardly knew.

"I'll come by your office for you at six," he said, and hung up the phone.

Hope found it difficult to concentrate for the rest of the day and retired to the ladies' room at ten minutes to six to comb her hair and refresh her makeup. She preferred not to examine her motives in doing so, instead preparing her arguments for Kirk's release. There was really no way Murphy could fight it, and Hope suspected he knew it. Murphy had been able to put Kirk away on questionable terms because the man was a repeat offender and indigent, unable to afford a private lawyer who would devote more time to his case than a harried and overworked P.D. As she retraced her mouth with lipstick, Hope resolved to make it clear that she was not going to be talked out of her intentions.

When Murphy arrived, Hope was waiting for him in the hall, her sweater over her arm and her briefcase in hand. He surveyed her unsmiling face and said dryly, "Where's the funeral?"

Hope didn't know how to respond. Did he think that a kidding tone would make her forget her mission?

"We have serious business to discuss," she finally said, returning his gaze steadily.

"I understand that. And if by chance I didn't, I'm sure you'd find a way to bring it home to me."

Hope was puzzled. The man had hardly spoken to her since the night of Sue's bar-passing celebration, and now he seemed to be acting offended that she was adopting a professional attitude toward this meeting.

"Ready to go?" she said, changing the subject.

He didn't answer, but led the way to his car. They passed Sue in the hall, and she looked after them thoughtfully.

"Am I going to get another civil liberties lecture?" he asked as he held the car door for her.

"No, but you're not going to talk me out of following through with this case."

He accepted that in a silence which continued until they were seated at the restaurant. As the waiter handed them their menus, he placed a card labeled with the number 17 against the bud vase on their table.

"What's that?" Murphy asked.

"We run a contest every Thursday night—free meal and a bottle of champagne if you win."

Murphy rolled his eyes, then ignored the placard as he leaned back in his chair and said, "Let me tell you about Robert Kirk."

Hope folded her hands on the table before her.

"You look like a bright fourth-grader in social-studies class," Murphy said to her, amused.

"Well, you're about to instruct me, aren't you?"

"I think there are some things you need to know."

Hope waited.

"Kirk is a sociopath."

"You said that already."

"It bears repeating. He hates everybody, has no regard for anyone's welfare except his own, and he expresses his feelings of economic and societal powerlessless through acts of violence against women," Murphy said bluntly.

"So you're saying we should keep him behind bars on any pretext—even an unlawful one?"

Murphy shrugged. "Draw your own conclusions."

"You want me to drop this inquiry, don't you?"

"I want you to think very carefully before you raise an issue that could put Kirk back on the streets."

"So you do think he'll get out if I pursue this," Hope said, pressing her point.

"It's a technicality, but it could work. The judges are all very cautious since the mayor put this review plan into action."

"Have you known about this all along?" Hope asked quietly, studying his face.

"What?"

"That Kirk was wrongfully imprisoned."

Murphy surveyed her narrowly. "I knew he was in prison. That's all I cared to know. Prison is where he belongs."

"May I bring you something to drink?" a cultured voice said at his elbow.

"Scotch, neat," Murphy said gruffly.

The server looked at Hope.

"Mineral water," Hope said.

"Afraid you'll get drunk and throw yourself at me?" Murphy said acerbically.

Hope ignored him.

"No, I can't imagine that ever happening," Murphy muttered, answering his own question.

"I want to keep a clear head," she finally said.

"To cross swords with me?"

"Something like that."

"I'm not that formidable."

"I think those you put behind bars would disagree."

Their drinks arrived and Murphy took a long swallow of his. Then he withdrew from his breast pocket a folded sheet ripped from a yellow legal pad.

"I took some notes from Kirk's court-ordered psychiatric review in his sealed juvenile records. You wouldn't have access to this through your computer and I had to get a writ of mandamus from Judge Kendall to open the file."

"I see you came prepared," Hope said.

"I thought you might see reason if I shared a few of these tidbits with you."

"I'm not promising anything."

"Of course not." Murphy cleared his throat. "Kirk first came to the attention of the authorities at the age of twelve, when he was turned in by a teacher for torturing and killing a stray dog on the school playground. He had apparently lured the pooch onto the tarmac with the promise of food, then inflicted suffering on it for a while for his own amusement before setting it on fire."

Hope swallowed, but held his gaze. She knew the point he was making. Cruelty to animals and children was universally regarded as a very bad sign.

Murphy rattled the sheet he held. "He apparently graduated from such activities to making threats of violence to some of his high school classmates. He was eventually removed from that environment and placed in juvenile hall for menacing one of his female teachers with a knife."

Hope fiddled with her fork.

"Shall I continue?"

"Please do," Hope responded quietly.

"Once he reached majority, he really flowered in his true calling. His first adult charge came about when a witness turned him in for sexually abusing a mentally retarded neighborhood girl." Murphy paused for effect. "He was apparently burning her breasts with a lit cigarette."

"May I take your order?" their waiter said.

"I'm not very hungry," Hope said faintly.

"Two Mediterranean salads, and we'll split a fisherman's platter," Murphy said to the man, who nodded and left.

"Okay with you?" Murphy asked her, raising one dark eyebrow in inquiry.

"I don't care."

"Shall I continue?" Murphy asked archly.

"It's really not necessary. I think you've made your point," Hope replied wearily.

"Any further questions about the solid citizen you're looking to turn loose on an unsuspecting world?"

"I'm not making an argument for his character, Dennis, but for the fairness of the legal system."

It was the first time she had used his given name, and she saw it register on his face.

"I guess what I'm saying is, overlook this one," he said in a low tone. "You can pursue other cases and still come up roses in the Mayor's eyes. Don't put Kirk back into society. He's too dangerous."

"You're asking me to compromise my position," Hope said, leaning across the table.

"No, I'm not. I'm asking you to use your head and keep a threat to our fellow citizens behind bars."

Hope shook her head stubbornly. "That's not the way I see it," she said levelly.

"If you had ever dealt with one of these creeps on a personal level, you wouldn't have such a high-and-mighty tone about it," Murphy said testily. "I'm familiar with your so-called constitutional cases. Filing suit because a minority worker was passed over for a promotion or barred from an affirmative-action program is not the same thing as springing a violent criminal from jail."

"I understand that."

"Do you? I don't think so. You've spent the last several years sitting in your nice, clean law office looking up case precedents and getting advice from ivory-tower academics on presenting your arguments. I guess what you need is to spend one night down in the tank with some of these poor, oppressed citizens you're so eager to help for reality to penetrate your consciousness."

"I think this meeting is over," Hope said crisply shoving back her chair to stand.

Murphy stood also. "Wait," he said.

"Why should I? Taking your abuse is not part of my job description. You've made your case—there's nothing further to say."

"But you haven't eaten."

"I have plenty of food at home." She started to walk past him and he touched her arm.

"Please stay," he said.

She hesitated.

"I'm sorry if I went too far. Your dinner will be here soon. It would be a shame to waste it."

As if in response to his words, their waiter started down the aisle from the kitchen bearing a tray.

"Here it is," Murphy said, as the waiter set up a serving stand and began to shift plates from it onto their table.

Hope sat again reluctantly, avoiding Murphy's eyes. She waited until the waiter had finished serving their meal and left, then said, "I'm sorry that you have such a low opinion of my position in your office, but I'm going to do my job, no matter what you think."

"That's becoming very clear to me," he said flatly.

"I'm glad that we understand each other," she said, picking up her fork and playing with her salad.

"I wish you wouldn't do that," Murphy said.

Hope glanced up. "What?"

"Stare down at your plate so you won't have to look at me," he replied.

Hope reddened slightly but didn't reply.

"I promise I'll drop the subject of Robert Kirk and try to be a pleasant dinner companion."

"Thank you."

"So," he said, after a pause, "how about those Phillies?"

Hope smiled slightly, and he grinned. He had a wonderful grin, open and mischievous and fun. Her own smile widened.

"Why did you become a lawyer?" he asked, out of the blue, lifting a flounder fillet from the platter in the center of the table and putting it on her plate.

"My father was a lawyer. I used to go to his office when I was a little kid and listen to him deal with his clients. It seemed like he was helping them, an admirable way to make a living. He died when I was in college, and I switched my major from education to pre-law a week later."

"Were you an only child?"

"Yes. I had a younger brother who died ten days after he was born, so my mother focused all her attention on me. She still does."

"She never remarried?"

"No."

"That places quite an emotional burden on you, doesn't it?" Murphy asked.

Hope gazed at him, surprised by his perception. "Yes," she said shortly.

"Is she after you to get married, provide her with grandchildren?" he inquired.

Hope didn't answer.

"Am I getting too personal?"

"Perhaps," she said mildly.

"All right. Let's change the subject. What do you think of your job so far?"

"I don't know if I should discuss that with you."

"Okay. But is it fair to say that you're not turning up as many cases of abuse of process as you thought you would?"

Hope shook her head, smiling.

"Ah, you're such a lawyer," he said, sighing, and took another sip of his drink.

Suddenly the band, which was tucked off to the side of the main room and had been playing softly, started to blast a loud fanfare. The maître d' descended on their table with their waiter and several other servers in tow.

"What the hell is this?" Murphy muttered.

A spotlight switched on and bathed them in a harsh, buttery glow.

"I feel like we're on *Let's Make a Deal*," Hope replied, glancing around them.

"Congratulations to our lucky couple number 17," the bandleader said into his mike. "They're our winners for tonight's free meal and bottle of champagne. Let's have a round of applause for them. And remember, you can be winners, too, just by dining with us every Thursday night. We have our draw at 8:00 p.m. sharp, so don't be late. And now, a dance for our winners. Lets join them in our own personal rendition of Nino Rota's 'Love Theme' from the 1968 motion picture *Romeo and Juliet*."

All the other patrons, clapping, had turned to stare at Murphy and Hope, who were trapped in the glare of the spotlight like deer in the headlights of a car.

"I guess we'd better do this," Murphy said, rising and extending his hand to Hope, who had no choice but to take it. They walked out onto the empty dance floor, and Murphy pulled Hope into his arms.

She tried to remember where they were, and their audience, but the sensation of being enveloped in his embrace was so wonderful that all other considerations seemed to fade into the background. He was so much taller than she was that her cheek was pressed against the lapel of his suit, an unusual situation for

Hope, who was generally at eye level with most men. His arms, which pulled her along through the steps effortlessly, tightened as the music swelled around them. Hope drifted along dreamily, her eyes closing luxuriously.

When the number finally ended, Murphy didn't release her for several seconds, finally letting her go when the spotlight switched off and the bandleader said, "There you go, folks. Our lucky winners for this evening, and don't they make a handsome couple? Thank you very much."

They went back to the table and sat in silence while the waiter uncorked the champagne, poured them each a glass, then stuck the bottle in a silver bucket of ice at Murphy's side.

"Enjoy," the waiter said, draping his napkin through the ring on the side of the ice bucket before he left.

"Well, that was embarrassing," Hope finally said, desperate to fill the silence.

"Oh, I don't know. It felt good to win something. The last contest I won was the drawing for the door prize at my fourth-grade Christmas party."

"What was it?"

"A year's subscription to *Boys' Life* magazine." He eyed her speculatively. "This was much more fun."

"You're a good dancer."

"Thanks. My wife taught me," he said shortly.

Something in his voice warned her that she should not pursue that subject.

The maître d' appeared, carrying a portable phone. "District Attorney Murphy?" he said.

"Yes."

"Your office is on line two."

Murphy accepted the phone, saying to Hope, "I left word that I would be here."

He punched a button and barked, "Murphy." Hope watched him as he listened and then said, "I'll be there in twenty minutes." He put the phone down on the table and gestured for the check.

"What is it?"

"Homicide in Germantown. The cops already have a suspect in custody. They want me to supervise the questioning to make sure they don't blow it." He smiled at her. "Wouldn't want somebody like you to look over the record six months from now and decide there might be grounds for an appeal."

Hope felt the good mood produced by the dance dissipating as Murphy paid the bill.

"I'll take you home," he said.

"Don't be ridiculous. I can take a cab."

"I brought you here, I'll bring you back. Your place is on the way." He stood and pulled out her chair.

Hope followed him out to the valet stand where they picked up his car. As they settled inside it and drove away, he said, "I hope you'll give some consideration to what I said tonight."

"I'll give it consideration."

"But your mind is already made up?"

"Don't start this again, Dennis."

"Maybe I should bring you along to see this homicide. It could give you some for food for thought about what your friend Kirk might be up to soon if you get him out."

"I'm not going to dignify that with a reply," Hope said tersely, looking out the window deliberately.

They drove the rest of the way in their usual traveling silence. When they reached Hope's building,
Murphy said, "Do you want me to walk you up to
your apartment?"

"That won't be necessary," Hope replied stiffly.

"Good night, then," he said neutrally, reaching
across her to open her door. She leaned back out of his
reach, then ten seconds later was standing on the curb
watching his car drive out of sight, feeling empty and
alone.

"Did you read the file?" Hope demanded of Meg
who was struggling through the door, balancing her
briefcase, her handbag, and a sack of groceries.

"Will you let me sit down first?" Meg countered
dumping her burdens on Hope's coffee table and then
staggering the few feet to the sofa, where she col-
lapsed.

"Fine. You're sitting. What did you think?" Hope
asked, dropping into the recliner across the way from
her.

"I think that Robert Kirk is one bad actor, just like
Murphy said," Meg replied, kicking off her shoes.

"No, I mean about the review. Do you think there
are grounds for an appeal?"

Meg looked at Hope soberly, then said, "Yes."

"How about the others on the advisory committee? Will they agree with you?"

Meg nodded. "Probably."

Hope received that news without comment, her expression thoughtful.

"You don't seem very happy," Meg observed. "I
thought you would be pleased."

"I guess that some part of me was hoping you wouldn't find any merit in the case," Hope admitted.

"Why? So you might not have to go head-to-head with Murphy over it?"

"If it wasn't this case, it would be another one. He thinks his office can do no wrong and everybody who gets a parking ticket should be sentenced to the electric chair."

"Oh, dear. It sounds like you had a nifty time at the restaurant the other night."

"Actually, parts of it weren't bad. But it ended on a decidedly sour note."

"Why?"

"He thinks he can bully me into changing my mind about the Kirk case. He recited to me all the grisly details of Kirk's juvy record, which you can well imagine, having seen the rest of it."

"So what's the point he's trying to make? Creeps aren't entitled to due process?"

"That's about the size of it."

"What are you going to do?"

"Well, since Murphy's going to fight this one like a tiger, I'm going to make sure all the others *do* agree with me before I present it to the mayor. I'll send them copies of the file tomorrow."

"Smart move."

"And if they respond as we expect, I'll recommend that Kirk's case be given a judicial review."

"He could get out immediately on time served if the previous verdict is vacated."

"I know that."

"And so does Murphy."

"You bet."

"Don't you think this is getting to be a personal thing with the two of you?"

"It seems it always was."

"What do you mean?"

"From day one, Murphy took it as an affront that his office was being investigated. And he's consistently viewed me as some kind of Pollyanna flake who wants to fling wide the prison doors and turn the felons loose on the world."

"That's just his job. It comes with the territory. D.A.s see only the worst element of the population and eventually they come to feel that they have to protect society from the offenders they *know* are doing horrible things."

"You sound like you're defending him."

Meg sighed. "Murphy knows Kirk. He's seen him face-to-face and heard him talk, experienced his attitude. I don't have to tell you that some of these people leave a very bad taste in the mouth. Murphy may really feel that he's warning you away from trouble."

Hope bit her lip. "What would you do?"

"Always let your conscience be your guide."

"Who's that? Mother Teresa?"

"Jiminy Cricket," Meg said, and grinned.

"Very funny. What did you bring for dinner?"

"*Tortellini a la panna.* You boil the water for the pasta. I brought a container of sauce from the gourmet store."

"Sounds like a lovely diet meal," Hope said, getting up and heading for the kitchen.

"Aren't you tired of tuna and salads?" Meg asked.

"Yes, but neither can I afford to buy a new wardrobe."

"We'll do four miles on the treadmill Saturday," Meg said, rising to join her.

"That's if Murphy doesn't break my legs tomorrow," Hope replied gloomily.

"Have you made up your mind, then? It sounds like you're planning to tell him what he doesn't want to hear."

"I have to follow through on this, Meg. I would be shirking my duty if I don't."

Meg nodded and reached into the overhead cupboard to locate the colander.

"If I can be of any help to you, let me know," she said, and Hope smiled.

The next day, Hope set her plan into motion, and three weeks later Kirk's case came up for judicial review. His previous verdict was vacated and a date set for a new trial on the old assault charge. Kirk was released on $25,000 bail—ten percent cash, posted by his mother. Hope was notified that Kirk had requested that she represent him for the new trial, since her term in the D.A.'s office would have expired by the date set for it.

Murphy stopped speaking to her entirely.

A few days after Kirk's release, Sue Chancellor knocked on the door of Hope's office and called, "May I come in?"

"It's open," Hope replied.

Sue entered and sat in the one spare chair the city had supplied with the office.

"I thought I should let you know that Robert Kirk has been calling the county bar registry, trying to get your home phone number," Sue said breathlessly.

"Swell," Hope said. "If he wants to get in touch with me about his case, why doesn't he call me here?"

"If I were in his shoes, I wouldn't be dialing this number. He's persona non grata around here, Hope."

"Well, so am I, since this news broke. Murphy communicates with me only through you, and the others barely nod hello and goodbye. Suddenly I'm Miss Popularity."

"What did you expect?" Sue said, shrugging. "Kirk is well-known to this office—I wasn't aware of that when I first discussed him with you. It turns out he was famous long before I signed on here. Several of the assistants worked hard to put him away. They're not going to thank you for springing him."

"I'm beginning to understand how an internal affairs investigator must feel at a police station," Hope said unhappily.

"It's a dirty job..." Sue said, letting the fragment linger, and then chuckled.

"You don't seem to care."

"Hell, no. I'm leaving for the comfort of a private practice in Brooklyn. A couple more years in this place and I might turn into a vigilante, like Dennis."

"Does that happen to everyone eventually?"

"It's hard to avoid it. If you see nothing but criminals all day long, day in and day out, you start to think that everyone is a criminal." She glanced at her watch. "Oops, gotta go. I just thought you should know about Kirk."

"Thanks," Hope said. She went back to the computer file she had been reading as the door closed behind Sue.

Hope stayed late that day, catching up on some old records, and it was past six when she finally took the elevator down to the basement garage. The lot was almost deserted, with just a few cars parked some distance from hers, and she was fishing in her purse for her keys when a man stepped out from behind a cement pavilion and smiled at her, blocking her path to the exit.

Hope started and dropped her keys, staring at the stranger. He was about her height but very muscular, wearing tight jeans with a T-shirt rolled up to reveal tattoos on both biceps. His blond hair was cut in a buzz and he sported a dangling earring in his left ear.

"Hi," he said. "I'm Bob Kirk. I understand you're the little lady who busted me out of jail."

# Four

Hope stared back at Kirk, speechless.

"Aren't you even pleased to meet me?" Kirk asked, lopsided grin in place.

"Of course," Hope said, recovering. "I just didn't expect to meet you *here.*"

"Well, I didn't think it would be such a good idea to show up at your office upstairs—the D.A. and I don't exactly see eye to eye." His grin widened.

"How did you know I would be working late today?" Hope asked uneasily, looking around at the empty garage.

"I didn't. I've just been watching every day since I got out, waiting for the moment to catch you alone." He stared at her unblinkingly, still smiling.

Hope's uneasiness grew. "Well, this really isn't the place to discuss your case," she said briskly.

"Name the spot," he fired back instantly, still with that unnerving grin firmly in place.

"I don't have the time today," she said, trying again.

"Name the time."

He was boxing her in neatly, and Hope cast about desperately for an idea that would satisfy his demand and yet allow her the safety of a public place.

"I could make some room for you on Friday at four in the afternoon, if you'll meet me at Chauncey's." It was a scrubbed but sterile diner, family oriented, with a bustling, rather than intimate, atmosphere. "Do you know it?"

"Sure."

"I'll see you then. I'll bring a copy of your records with me, and I'd advise you to bring whatever you have—subpoenas, your bail documents, et cetera. Is that clear?"

He nodded, undressing her with his eyes.

"Well, I must be going," Hope said with a briskness she did not feel. She turned her back on him deliberately to unlock her car, waiting for him to seize her from behind, her heart thumping so loudly she was sure he could hear it. She forced herself to move slowly as she got in and started the car, not glancing at Kirk until she was past him and she could see him in the rearview mirror, looking after her with that smug expression she would never forget.

Hope ascended through the levels of the garage and presented her ticket at the gate. She glided through it and drove several blocks on automatic pilot before the adrenalin rush began to fade and she pulled over to the curb, trembling. She put her head down on the steering wheel and closed her eyes, taking several deep breaths before it occurred to her that Kirk might have a car and be following her. She bolted upright and looked straight into the steely gaze of a Philadelphia police officer, who had stopped his patrol car in front of her car.

Hope's heart began to pound again. The blue light on the police car was whirling silently. Thank God he hadn't activated the siren; she would have jumped right out of her skin.

"Is something wrong, miss?" he asked, his hand on the holster of his gun. Did he think she was some drug-crazed maniac? Then again, maybe his caution was justified. She could only imagine the look that must be on her face.

"Everything is fine, Officer. I just felt a little dizzy, that's all, and decided to pull over for a short rest."

"May I see your license and registration, please?" he said. Did they ever say anything else?

Hope reached for her purse on the seat and extracted her wallet from it with trembling fingers.

"Please remove them from the billfold," he said.

Hope did so, and also handed him her I.D. from the district attorney's office. He examined all three documents and then gave them back to her through the open window.

"You work with Dennis Murphy?" he asked.

"Not *with* him, exactly. I'm heading up the mayor's task force to oversee the D.A.'s office."

He studied her unsmilingly. "I read about it in the paper," he said, leaving no doubt about what he thought of her mission.

"May I go, Officer... Penshansky?" Hope asked, reading his name off his I.D. tag. "I'm really fine now, and I have to get home."

Penshansky stepped back from the car. "This is a bad place to stop, Miss Jarvis," he said. "If you need a rest in the future, I'd advise you to pull into a parking lot or get a spot at a meter."

*I'll remember that the next time I'm accosted by a serial rapist,* Hope thought. Aloud she said, "Thank you, Officer Penshansky, I'll bear it in mind."

Penshansky touched the peak of his cap. "Good night, Miss Jarvis. Drive carefully."

"Good night, Officer." Hope waited until he had gotten into his patrol car and pulled out before she surged ahead, falling into the lane behind him. At the first corner, she turned off to lose him, circling around to the same point and then driving home.

As she walked through the door to her apartment, the phone was ringing.

She knew it was her mother. Throughout her life, when she thought that nothing else could go wrong, something did, and it was usually her mother. Hope slumped on the sofa and let the phone ring, closing her eyes as the answering machine clicked on and she waited for her mother's flat Long Island accent to fill the room.

It was not her mother. A man's voice said, "This is Bob Kirk. I just wanted to say how nice it was to meet you and I'm looking forward to seeing you again on Friday."

Hope sat bolt upright, a sinking feeling growing in her stomach. How had he gotten her home phone number? It was unlisted, and the bar registry would never have given it to him, no matter how much he pestered them.

Hope got up and shut off the machine, trying not to let fear overwhelm her and wondering what to do. Should she contact the police? Kirk had done nothing actionable, and antagonizing him over a visit and a phone message was surely not a bright idea.

Hope dialed Meg's number and hung up when Meg's voice, on an answering machine, began to give her spiel.

She went into the kitchen to get a drink of water and resolved to discuss it with Sue at work.

Sue might know what to do.

"So, to what do I owe this magnificent repast?" Sue said jokingly to Hope, gesturing at the chicken salad sandwich and glass of ice tea sitting on the table before her. They were having lunch at Hope's invitation.

"I have to ask your advice on something, and I didn't want to do it at the office," Hope said.

"Fire away," Sue told her, lifting the sandwich and taking a bite of it.

"Robert Kirk cornered me in the underground garage last night as I was leaving, and then called my apartment when I got home. I was wondering if I should do anything about it."

Sue put down the sandwich and stared at Hope.

"Don't look at me that way. I'm asking for your advice on what to do, not a judgment on my foolish behavior."

"You'd better tell Murphy right away," Sue said.

Hope groaned. "I was afraid you were going to say that."

"I mean it, Hope. I know he can be a pain in the neck, but if Robert Kirk were stalking me I'd want Murphy on my side."

"Kirk's not stalking me."

"What do you call it?"

"He wants me to represent him."

"Bull. He must have gone to some trouble to get your number, and through some devious means. You know what a dangerous character he is, so why are you even entertaining the idea of taking him on as a client?"

"What should I say?"

"Say anything, for God's sake. Tell him you're overbooked, you're about to be disbarred, you're expiring of a terminal illness. What difference does it make?"

"He's going to see through any of those stories."

"So what? Get rid of him."

"And make him angry? What do you think will happen then?"

Sue took a long pull on her ice tea. "I'm telling you, get Murphy in on this."

"He's just going to give me a lecture."

"No, he won't. When you're really in trouble he's a godsend, believe me."

It occurred to Hope, not for the first time, that Sue was half in love with her boss.

"If you don't tell him, I will," Sue added challengingly, picking up her sandwich and taking another bite.

"You wouldn't! I told you this in confidence!" Hope protested, outraged.

Sue waved her hand deprecatingly. "Are you going to let your pride place you in danger? I'm not."

Hope tried to stare her down, but Sue met her gaze unflinchingly, chewing methodically.

"Today," Sue said, "or I will."

In the end the decision was made for Hope—Murphy was waiting for her at her office door when they returned from lunch.

"May I have a moment?" he said to Hope, and Sue glanced meaningfully at Hope, as if to say, Now's the time.

"See you later, Hope," Sue said airily, and she ambled lazily down the hall.

"Have you recovered the power of speech?" Hope said sarcastically to Murphy as he followed her into her office and then shut the door. "I thought you had gone mute."

"I went to a Policeman's Beneficial Association benefit last night," he said, ignoring her comment. "I ran into Joe Penshansky there."

"Who's Joe—" Hope began, and then she remembered. The cop on Market Street.

"He tells me he stopped you yesterday."

"He didn't stop me, I was already stopped. I don't understand what it has to do with you."

"When he saw that you worked in this office he thought I might like to know that you looked faint, as if you might pass out at the wheel and have an accident."

"That's ridiculous. I'm perfectly fine. Does he report to you every time he makes a routine inquiry? What is this—'Big Brother is watching you'?"

"What's going on, Hope?"

"I don't know what you mean."

"You're not the fainting type."

"How do you know what type I am?"

They were facing each other in the small room, body language indicating that the tension was running high. Murphy's arms were folded, his expression grim, and Hope's hands were clenched in a knot at her waist.

Finally Murphy sighed and said in a lower, conciliatory tone, "Are you going to tell me what happened?"

Something about this sudden concession undid her. Hope swallowed hard and said quietly, "Kirk was waiting for me in the underground garage when I came off work last night."

All the color drained from Murphy's face, leaving him pale beneath his spring tan. "Did he hurt you?" he asked hoarsely.

Hope shook her head. "He just talked, said how nice it was to finally meet me. But it was his attitude...." She shivered.

"What attitude?" Murphy demanded, his blue eyes glittering like chips of ice.

"Insinuating. That smile... you'd have to see it."

"I have seen it. Did he say anything else?"

"He wants me to represent him at his new trial."

"And?"

"I agreed to meet him at Chauncey's on Friday."

"What?" Murphy exploded. He looked as if he were going to hit her. "Do you have a death wish or something? I can't believe this—you must be out of your mind!''

"It's a public place."

"You shouldn't have agreed to meet him in Times Square at high noon or in the middle of the St. Patrick's Day Parade! This man is dangerous, must I repeat myself? You should have told him you couldn't represent him!"

"I didn't want to make him angry."

"You don't seem to mind making me angry!" he countered, thrusting his hands through his hair.

"You don't have his interesting arrest record."

"Oh, so now you're afraid? A little late in the game, isn't it?" He was so exasperated, he could hardly look at her. He began pacing up and down in the narrow space, causing her to dodge out of his way.

"Tell me exactly what happened," Murphy finally said, whirling to face her.

Hope recounted both episodes, the meeting in the garage and the phone call.

"Very clever," Murphy muttered. "He's smart—he hasn't done anything we could have him picked up for. There's no crime." He smiled coldly. "If I did have him arrested, somebody like you would spring him inside five minutes and he'd be suing us for false arrest in the bargain."

Hope said nothing. He was right.

Murphy leaned against her desk and surveyed her archly. "Well, this is another fine mess you've gotten us into," he said.

"Us?"

"I seem to be standing here with you."

"What should I do?" Hope asked.

"It's what I'll do. I'm going with you to meet him."

"You can't do that!" Hope gasped. "He'll be furious— He hates you. You put him away."

He stared at her so long she finally reddened and looked away from him.

"All right, I screwed up. I'm sorry," she said.

"You have to tell him that you can't take his case."

"Why? What reason can I give?"

"Tell him you have no interest in pursuing his case."

"After I spent all that time and energy getting him released? I'll need a lot of helium to get a brick-lined blimp like that one off the ground."

"Tell him anything—what does it matter?" Murphy said, echoing Sue's advice. "The point is, once you break off the professional relationship we *can* have him picked up if he continues to bother you, detains you physically or restrains your liberty. He'll have no excuse for the contact."

"Dennis, I understand you're trying to help me, but you can't come with me. I don't know what he'll do if he sees you."

Murphy mulled that over, rolling his lower lip between his teeth. "Then let me send one of the assistants with you, someone he won't recognize. Dave Clendon—he's a big, burly guy, knows how to handle himself. He's a tae kwon do master. We can say that Dave's your assistant."

Hope nodded eagerly, glad that he was listening to reason.

"I'd like to send some undercover police protection, but on this flimsy evidence I'd never get authorization," he murmured, thinking out loud.

"I understand." He looked at her, and Hope faced him squarely. "I really appreciate your helping me out with this," she said.

He shook his head. "Friday may not be the end of it, you know. He's unlikely to give up so easily."

"I know."

"We'll have to take it one step at a time. Let me talk to Dave and I'll get back to you." He turned for the door.

Hope stepped in front of him and put her hand on his arm. "Thanks, Dennis."

He touched her chin with his thumb, the first time he had ever touched her affectionately.

"You're going to drive me crazy," he said, and then opened her door and left.

It seemed a very long time until Friday, and then the day itself was an eternity. When Dave Clendon finally came to Hope's office at three-forty-five, she was re-arranging her briefcase for the second time. Anything to keep busy.

"Ready?" Dave said. He was a strapping six-footer who looked more like a football tackle than an attorney.

"Yes."

"Don't worry about a thing. He's not going to pull any stunts with me there," Dave said reassuringly.

*But you're not always going to be there,* Hope thought. What she needed was a bodyguard. And it was not comforting to know that she was responsible for her own predicament.

She had set Kirk loose on the world.

Kirk was waiting at the diner when they got there; his cocky smile faded when he saw Dave Clendon with Hope.

"Hello, Mr. Kirk. This is my assistant, David Clendon. He came along to take notes as we discuss your case," Hope said neutrally, as she slid into the booth across from Kirk.

Dave extended his hand. Kirk ignored it.

"You didn't tell me you were bringing him," Kirk said dully, as Dave sat next to Hope.

"We work as a team," Hope lied smoothly.

Kirk glared at Dave but said nothing.

Hope went through a routine review of his case as Dave dutifully scribbled on a notepad and asked a few questions of his own. Kirk was clearly not happy but was forced to go along with the charade he had initiated. After about an hour, Hope closed her briefcase smartly and said, "I think that's enough for today, Mr. Kirk. I'll review what I have here and then I'll be back in touch to let you know if I can handle your retrial."

Kirk's mouth fell open unattractively. "What do you mean? I thought you already agreed to represent me."

"I agreed to *consider* it. I have to weigh how much preparation time will be required and then see if I can fit it into my schedule."

His eyes grew flat and hard, and he looked from Hope to Dave measuringly. Then he stood.

"I have money," he said sneeringly to Hope, "if that will persuade you. My mother sold her house to raise money for my retrial." Then he strolled down the aisle of the diner, and through the window they saw him exit the doors and trot down the steps.

"Charming guy," Dave said, taking a long sip of the glass of ice water on the table. "Why do I feel like I need a bath?"

"How do you think it went?" Hope asked nervously.

"Fine. I told you he wasn't going to try anything with me along. He's a coward—they never get involved in a fair fight."

"He knew I brought you for protection," Hope said.

"So what?"

"He felt outmanuevered. He didn't like it."

"Forget him," Dave said. "He's like a bug that you scrape off your shoe. Call him next week and tell him you don't have time to represent him. End of story."

Hope didn't think so. Kirk's malevolent eyes had been full of unfinished business.

"Do you want to get something to eat?" Dave asked, picking up a menu.

Hope had never felt less hungry in her life.

Hope returned to her office and went on with her work, but she was wary, looking around every corner for Robert Kirk. When she called to tell him she couldn't be his lawyer, he listened in silence and then said, "Thanks a lot, bitch," and hung up the phone in her ear.

She did not find his response reassuring.

Murphy kept tabs on the situation, checking in with her every day, but for a while there was nothing to report. Hope tried to put the specter of Kirk out of her mind, and she had just about succeeded when she came home on a Friday evening two weeks after the meeting at Chauncey's.

She was anticipating a date with Meg's cousin, who had been asking her out for months. She had finally agreed to go to dinner with him, as much to forget her troubles as to get him off her back. She certainly needed some diversion, and she was thinking about taking a shower and washing her hair when she stepped out of her car in the parking lot behind her building. She bent over the back seat to get her brief-case when she was seized roughly, and a masculine hand clamped over her mouth.

"Hi," a harsh voice said in her ear. "Remember me?"

Hope knew immediately that it was Kirk. Flooded with panic, she had to struggle to remember her self-defense instructions. She went limp and offered no resistance.

"Thought you got rid of me, didn't you?" he sneered, pinning her arms behind her back. "Brought along that gorilla to our meeting and then dropped me like a hot potato. What's the matter, Counselor? Don't like the criminals to get too close?"

Tears sprang to Hope's eyes as he wrenched her into position against the hood of the car, holding her with his weight. "How do you feel now, Miss High-and-Mighty 'I don't have time for you' Jarvis?" he muttered. "Gonna let me have a little taste? Who've you been saving it up for?" He freed one hand and grabbed the neck of her blouse, wrenching it down-ward. The fabric split to her waist, revealing her lace-trimmed chemise, the tops of her breasts. He eyed her greedily, distracted for a second, and Hope tried to break free, kicking out at his legs. Enraged, he struck her across the face brutally, and she saw stars.

Then she was released so suddenly that she fell to her hands and knees on the blacktop. Dazed, she looked up to see Murphy pummeling a staggering and overmatched Kirk, who tried to fight back but was clearly losing the battle. Gathering the shreds of her tattered blouse around her, Hope tried to stand, but succeeded only in slumping against the side of her car. The muffled grunts and groans of the fighting men combined with the faint ringing in her ears to give an otherworldly aspect to the scene. How had Murphy gotten here? How had he known? she wondered in confusion as Murphy dealt a final crushing blow to Kirk's jaw, which sent the man reeling into the fender of Hope's car, to slide limply to the ground, out cold.

Murphy was at Hope's side in an instant. "Are you all right?" he gasped, picking her up and cradling her in his arms.

"I'm okay, I think," she whispered, clinging to him. "I was just so...scared." Then she started to cry.

He let her weep for a few minutes, smoothing her tangled hair back from her face, making soothing, shushing noises. When she had recovered enough to ask a question, she said, "How did you know?"

"I didn't. I just remembered his fondness for parking lots. I've been following you home every night for two weeks."

Hope gazed up at him in amazement as the building security guard, too late but briskly efficient, came charging around a corner. He stopped when he saw Kirk's prone form.

"I had a report of a disturbance," he said, glancing at Hope and Murphy for explanation.

"There was an attempted rape," Murphy said to him. "I'm District Attorney Murphy. I'm taking this lady up to her apartment. Please call the police. Can I leave this suspect in your custody?" Murphy pulled a card out of his jacket pocket and handed it to the guard, who looked suitably impressed, but still glanced apprehensively at Kirk. Hope's tormentor was about as threatening as a dead mackerel at the moment, and once the guard ascertained this, he puffed up with the importance of his mission as he said in a deep voice, "Certainly, sir."

"Do you carry handcuffs?"

"No, sir."

"Then tie him up with your belt and sit on him until the police arrive. You can use the phone in my car—it's right around the corner, the black sedan. The door's open."

"Yes, sir," the guard replied, moving to obey.

Hope lay in a dreamy lassitude against Murphy's shoulder, dimly aware of the ride up in the elevator and of him fishing in her purse for her keys. He strode across her living room and set her gently on the couch, pausing to pull the lap robe from her rocker over her knees.

"How do you feel?" he asked, as she opened her eyes to find him hovering, her phone in his hand.

"Numb. Distant."

He reached down to touch her mouth gingerly, and she winced with the pain.

"You're going to have a fat lip in the morning," he said ruefully. "It's already puffing up nicely."

Hope groaned and fell back against the sofa pillow, drawing the robe around her protectively. She was so cold, suddenly; she couldn't seem to stop shaking.

"Hugh, this is Dennis," Murphy said suddenly into the phone. "I'm calling you at six-forty-five Friday. Please get back to me at this number as soon as you can. It's an emergency, so hurry."

"Who were you calling?" Hope asked.

"My brother the doctor, the one who wrote you the prescription. He's never home, but he checks his messages every half hour."

"Why did you tell him it was an emergency?"

"Because it is. If you had a mirror you'd know it, too."

"Thanks a lot." Hope made an effort to think clearly. "Can you make a call for me?"

"Sure."

"I had a date tonight. The number's on the pad by the lamp. Please tell him I'm . . . indisposed . . . and I'll call in a few days to explain."

Murphy left the message and then came and sat next to her, peering into her face.

"Stop staring at me," she said faintly. "I can guess how I must look."

"You're pale as a sheet and shaking like the Third Avenue El with a train going over it. Do you have any brandy?"

"No."

"Well, what do you have to drink?"

"I don't know—look in that cabinet," Hope replied, gesturing toward her sideboard. He obeyed and pulled out a bottle.

"Raspberry liqueur?" he said, making a gagging face. "Where did you get this stuff?"

"Christmas present. I don't drink."

"So I've noticed. Why not?"

"My grandfather—my mother's father—was an alcoholic. My mother is paranoid on the subject. We never had booze in the house, not even on holidays. I just grew up without it and never got interested."

"Remind me never to offer your mom a snort," he said dryly. "Okay, Zelda, I guess we'll have to wait for the good doctor to call back." Then he pushed aside a pile of napkins and peered deeper into the cabinet. "Wait a minute. Here's an unopened bottle of scotch. Covered with dust. When did you get this?"

"I don't know," Hope replied, shivering. "House-warming, I think, when I moved in here."

"When Coolidge moved into the White House, you mean. There's moss growing on the north side of it." He pulled off the seal and walked into the kitchen. Hope heard the sound of liquid being poured into a glass, and he returned with one of her cut-glass tumblers half-filled with a brown fluid.

"Drink this down," he instructed.

Hope tried, and she managed several large sips before she closed her eyes and shook her head.

"No more."

"It will help, I promise."

"Don't make me drink any more. Please," she whispered. A tear squeezed out from under one lid and she looked away. He sat next to her on the couch again and gathered her into his arms. Too drained to pro-test, and remembering the comfort of his earlier embrace, Hope submitted, dropping her head against his shoulder and closing her eyes.

"I'm sorry," Murphy murmured, settling her comfortably into the curve of his body. "I thought if I kept you talking, got your mind off it..." He let the sentence trail into silence, tucking the lap robe more closely around her.

"Told you so," Hope said, feeling the warmth of the liquor stealing through her body.

"What?"

"Aren't you going to say 'I told you so'?"

"No."

"Why not?" Her voice was fading to a mumble.

"I'm too relieved that you're all right," he replied, and that was the last thing she remembered before she fell asleep.

When Hope awoke, there were three men sitting in her living room, all of them staring at her. There was a pillow under her head and Murphy was nowhere in sight.

"Where's Dennis?" she asked, struggling to a sitting position and looking from one to the other of her visitors.

"He's on the phone in the bedroom," said the man who looked vaguely like Murphy. There was a blood-pressure cuff in his hand, and Hope made the brilliant deduction that this was Hugh, the doctor. The other two men were uniformed policemen.

"I'm Hugh Murphy," the first one said. "These two officers are waiting to question you. I want to check you over and make sure you're fit for the interview before they do."

"I'm fit enough to give a police report," Hope said, sitting up straighter.

"Let me be the judge of that." He took her blood pressure, counted her pulse and examined the cut on her face. Then he stepped back and said to the cops, "All right. You can talk to her if you want."

The taller policeman stood up and took out a notebook. "I'm Officer Shostak and this is Officer Dillon," he said.

Hope nodded at the two men.

"We'd like you to tell us exactly what happened from the moment Kirk accosted you, until District Attorney Murphy arrived."

Hope recounted the episode to the best of her recollection, as Shostak asked pertinent questions and recorded her answers. The inquisition was mercifully brief, with only one really uncomfortable moment.

"So there was no penetration?" Shostak asked, scribbling away, not glancing at her.

"No," Hope replied, her face flaming as Hugh Murphy looked on expressionlessly. "He ripped my blouse and chemise, yanked at my skirt. I mean, he was trying, but..."

"But Murphy broke it up?" Shostak asked, finally pausing in his writing to meet her gaze.

She nodded, mortified.

"There's nothing to be embarrassed about, Miss Jarvis," Shostak said smoothly. "Rape is a crime of violence, and you're an innocent victim."

Hope nodded again.

Shostak closed his notebook and said, "I think that's all. I'm not sure what we'll be charging him with yet, probably first-degree assault and aggravated sexual assault in addition to attempted rape. We'll talk it over with D.A. Murphy. But I'd have to say that you're one lucky lady. If Murphy hadn't arrived, I don't want to think about what might have happened to you."

Hope did not reply. She knew he was right, but didn't feel very lucky at the moment.

Murphy came out of her bedroom and joined them, saying, "Booking is waiting for him. It's all set. You gentlemen through?"

Shostak nodded.

"Hugh, you take care of her," Murphy said to his brother. "I'm going to walk out with these guys."

Hugh exchanged a meaningful glance with his brother, but said nothing.

When the three men were outside the apartment and beyond Hope's earshot, Murphy said to the cops, "How did it go?"

"Fine. She was coherent. Shaken up, you know, but otherwise okay. A lot better than some I've seen who've had similar experiences," Shostak replied.

"Isn't she the one assigned to your office for some investigation?" Dillon asked. "From the mayor's office?"

"Yes."

"Then she got Kirk out of jail!" Dillon said, looking wonderingly at his partner. "I was reading about it in the paper. She's got nobody to blame for this but herself!"

Murphy grabbed Dillon by the lapel and said tightly, "She was doing her job, Officer Dillon, and I would appreciate it if you wouldn't share that piece of information with anybody else."

Dillon stared at him, shocked into silence, and Murphy released him abruptly.

"I want to keep this as quiet as possible—closed arraignment, no press," Murphy added. "I know she'll have to be present to identify him, but I'm a witness, too, and I'd consider it a favor if you'd direct everything that you can through me."

Dillon didn't answer at all, so Shostak interjected quickly, "Sure Murph."

"Thanks, guys. I'd better get back in there." He walked away and left the two policemen staring after him.

"What the hell was that about?" Dillon said, amazed.

"What do you need, George—skywriting? Can't you see he's got a case on that girl?"

"Murphy?" Dillon said, a slow grin spreading across his face. "I don't believe it."

"Hey, it happens."

"Not to him! The iron man hasn't even had a date since his wife died. At least, that's the word around town."

"Well, I think that's about to change. Didn't you get a look at her in there? I know she's a mess right now, but that's one fine-looking woman. And they're working together every day, all day—you don't have to be Einstein to figure it out."

Dillon chuckled.

"Come on," Shostak said, smiling, too. "We have to get back to the precinct."

Murphy walked back into Hope's apartment as Hugh was writing a prescription for a tranquilizer.

"I don't want that," Hope was saying.

"She can't have that," Murphy said.

Hugh looked from one to the other, brows raised, as if they were a comedy team.

"I already gave her liquor," Murphy added.

"What are you doing now—practicing medicine without a license?" Hugh inquired of his brother.

"I gave her a drink to settle her down."

"As they do in all the best old movies," Hugh said dryly, taking off his glasses and stowing them in his pocket. He handed the slip of paper to his brother.

"I won't need a tranquilizer," Hope said.

"You may not think so now, but sometimes these episodes have aftereffects. In a few days you may feel...unsettled...or you may not be able to sleep. Just follow the directions on the bottle."

Hope sighed and nodded obediently.

"And if you feel in need of counseling, someone to talk to, I can recommend a woman, a psychologist—"

"Thank you," Hope said crisply, cutting him short. "I know several people with the Rape Crisis Center in town."

"Oh yes, of course," Hugh said deferentially. He looked around for his bag. "I'd better be leaving."

"Thanks for coming," Hope said automatically.

"Can I speak to you a moment?" Hugh said pointedly to his brother, who followed him into the hall.

Hope lay back against the pillow and closed her eyes resignedly. All these hole-in-corner conversations were getting on what nerves she had left.

"What's going on?" Hugh said to Murphy in the hall.

"What do you mean?"

"Isn't this the same girl you got the burn salve for not too long ago?"

"Yes."

"What is she—accident prone?"

"That isn't funny."

Hugh put his hand on his brother's arm. "Denny, are you involved with her?"

"No. I mean, not the way you mean."

"That's very clear."

"I'm not sleeping with her, all right?" Murphy said in exasperation, his hands on his hips.

"But you want to, right? Desperately."

Murphy didn't answer.

"I think I have a right to ask."

"Do you?"

"Come on, Denny. I know what you went through when Claire died. After that you put up walls no woman could knock down. How many dates did I try to arrange for you? How many dates did everyone else you know try to arrange for you? Now I see you hovering around this girl like Florence Nightingale, it makes me wonder."

"Is that what bothers you? That I found her on my own?" Murphy countered, amused.

"Found her? So you *are* hung up on her?"

"Maybe."

"Does she know?"

"She is, undoubtedly, the most obtuse and gratuitously stubborn woman I have ever met."

"I see."

"I thought about dating her once before, when she was in law school. I asked around, found out she was engaged, so I didn't take it any further. Then she moved away and Claire happened. But when I saw Hope turn up a few years ago, it was always in the back of my mind. I watched her, thought about her, just never worked up the nerve to do anything about it."

"Then the mayor sicced her on you," Hugh said.

"Right."

"What are you going to do?"

"I don't know."

"Don't press her now. After her experience to-night . . ."

Murphy stared at him.

"All right, all right," Hugh said quickly. "I understand. You know better than that. But this whole thing with Kirk has to remind you of what happened to Claire, and I'm worried."

Murphy was silent, his expression grim.

Hugh glanced at his watch. "I'm late," he said. "Are you sure you don't want me to treat those abrasions for you? Just a little peroxide and iodine—your knuckles are scraped raw. And you're going to have a shiner in the morning."

Murphy smiled. Hugh in his physician mode always reminded him of their mother. She was a natural caretaker, too.

"I told you already—no. I'll just take a shower and I'll be fine. Go on home. Say hello to Marsha and the kids. And thanks for coming over here."

Hugh patted his brother's shoulder and headed for the elevator. Murphy went back inside and said to Hope, "How are you?"

"A lot older than when you left," she replied. "What were you two talking about?"

"Oh, family things, you know," he replied vaguely. "How are you feeling?"

"Nervous."

"About what?"

"Staying here alone tonight."

That gave him pause.

"Meg is out of town and my neighbor Peggy is on vacation. I'd rather call Dracula than my mother..." she began.

"Are you hinting that you want me to stay the night with you?" he said.

# Five

---

Hope's eyes widened, horrified at what she'd implied. Could she be drunk? On two ounces of liquor taken several hours earlier? Some peculiar things were coming out of her mouth.

"That's not what I meant," she amended hastily.

He waited, watching her. She was still huddled under the lap robe like a refugee from the *Titanic*, and wearing approximately the same expression those disaster survivors must have had.

"I just feel . . . insecure," she said quietly. "I know it's silly. I know Kirk is in jail right now."

A lump formed in her throat. Murphy had every right to be furious with her, and instead he was sitting here playing nursemaid.

Sue was right. When you needed him, Murphy was a brick.

"I'm so tired," she whispered, her eyes filling again. Why couldn't she stop crying? She was helpless to control her emotions, a rare and disabling experience. The last time she had felt like this was when her father died.

"Let me help you into bed," he said. He took her arm as she stood, and when she stumbled, he picked her up and carried her into the bedroom. He didn't even turn on the light, just drew back the coverlet and set her down, then drew the comforter up to her chin.

"I'll sleep on the couch in the living room," he said, smoothing the blanket.

Hope tried to protest, but managed only a feeble gesture before she closed her eyes. Murphy waited until she was breathing evenly and then slipped out into the hall, shutting the door behind him.

His head was reverberating like a struck gong, and he went into the bathroom and searched the medicine cabinet for aspirin. His face in the mirror gave him a start. He looked like the self-portrait of van Gogh which had fascinated him as kid: the same disordered hair and wild gleam in the eye—the aftereffect, he guessed, of his homicidal rage toward Kirk.

He located a bottle of aspirin and swallowed three, washing them down with a tepid gush of tap water. Then he went into the living room and poured himself a stiff drink from Hope's sole bottle of potable liquor, sitting with it on the sofa where Hope had lately been and propping his feet on a hassock.

He had crossed some sort of boundary, and he knew it. He knew it when he'd found himself following Hope home every day to make sure she made it there safely; he knew it when he'd seen Kirk's hands on

Hope and felt, for the second time in his life, the urge to kill another human being. The first time had been when Claire died, and he had not expected to feel that deeply again. But it had happened.

Hope had always been able to get to him. He'd been fascinated when he first saw her during her moot-court competition, bitterly disappointed when he learned she was engaged. During his brief time with Claire, Hope's memory had faded to the background. But when she returned to the area and he began to see her at bar meetings and political functions, he felt the old pull return.

The fact that she seemed to be unaware of him did nothing to diminish its strength. And then, when she was assigned to oversee his office, his conflicting feelings about having his territory invaded by the object of his long-term desire did not make him pleasant company. No wonder she wouldn't listen to him.

He took a large swallow of his drink, feeling his headache recede to a tolerable level. What he really needed was a shower, but he was too tired to move. It would have to wait until morning. He thought about checking in with his office, but then decided that could wait until morning, too. He lay back against the pillow Hope had used and pulled her lap robe over him.

In seconds he was asleep.

Murphy woke about six o'clock a.m., disoriented in the unfamiliar room. He sat up and looked around, then remembered the events of the previous night. He stood, stumbled over the coffee table, and then moved quietly to Hope's bedroom, opening the door and glancing inside. She was still sleeping in the same position she had occupied when he'd left her. The bruise on her mouth was purpling and her upper lip was distorted; just seeing that made the rage swell within him again. It was a good thing Kirk was behind bars.

Murphy went back into the living room and called the precinct for the time of Kirk's arraignment, then checked his home answering machine, where he heard another cautionary message from Hugh. Smiling to himself as he hung up, he felt the need for coffee and went into the kitchen to search out the machine that Hope had used on his previous visit.

Luckily, it was in plain sight, with a stack of prepacks sitting right next to it. He made the coffee and then thought longingly of a shower once more. Should he wait until he got home? Was there really a reason to do so? Hope was asleep, and he knew he was unfit for civilized company. He would be out and dressed before she knew it. He decided to go ahead and carried his cup of coffee into the bathroom with him.

It was a feminine bower, with pink-and-green posy-printed wallpaper and a stack of fluffy pink towels filling a white wicker étagère against the wall. A mirrored dressing tray jammed with an assortment of crystal bottles sat on the vanity stand next to the sink. Feeling like a voyeur, he picked up a half-filled container shaped like a swan and sniffed the cap. It smelled like her. He put it back down hastily, as if it might burn him.

Murphy glanced at himself in the mirror; he looked marginally better than he had the night before, but now he was badly in need of a shave, and the dark beard gave him a sinister look that reminded him of his long-dead and unmourned father. Dismissing the thought, he frowned at the Lilliputian-sized silver razor sitting on the washstand and pulled back the shower curtain. He examined the mechanism, fiddling with the knobs until he got the water running into the tub at the right temperature. Then he pulled the plug and threw the lever that sent the water flooding from the overhead nozzle.

He was lathering himself with Hope's large pink bar of soap when he heard a noise from the next room. He cocked his head and turned off the water. Nothing. He resumed showering and was rinsing his hair when he heard it again. A whimper? He shut off the water and stepped out onto the floor, glancing at the pile of his discarded clothes and then grabbing a bath towel and wrapping it around his middle. He went into the hall and the sound was louder, coming from Hope's room. Without another thought he pulled her door open and walked into the bedroom.

Hope was having a nightmare, tossing and moaning, the bedclothes in a knot. He sat on the edge of the bed and took her hands, trying to rouse her. She continued to thrash and cry in her sleep, so he pulled her toward him and gathered her into his arms, murmuring into her ear. Soothed by the sound of his voice, she stopped struggling and opened her eyes. It was several seconds before she registered who he was, and then she flung her arms around his neck, collapsing against him in an ecstasy of relief. He rocked her back and forth as if she were a child.

"Kirk was here," she gasped.

"No, he wasn't. It was a dream," Murphy replied.

"It was so real." She shuddered.

"Yes, I know, I know," Murphy said, pulling her closer. It seemed the most natural thing in the world to press his lips to her neck, then the exposed skin of her shoulder. Hope sighed and relaxed into his embrace, her eyes closing again.

"You're all wet," she murmured.

"I was taking a shower," he said, his mouth moving lower. She was still wearing the chemise Kirk had ripped, and it exposed her breasts almost to the nipple. Murphy bent, one arm tight about her waist, and captured the rosy tip through the silken cloth, causing her to gasp and arch her back. With his free hand, he caressed her legs and then lifted her into his lap.

"I've wanted you for so long," he muttered, as she sank her hands into his damp hair, holding his head against her. She could feel his arousal against her thighs, filling her with a melting yearning.

"Since I came to work with you?" she whispered, awash in the sensations his mouth was evoking.

"Before," he muttered. "Long before." He shifted his weight and his towel fell to the floor as he lay her flat on the bed. She pulled him down to her, as his cheek, rough with stubble, pressed against hers. He bent to kiss her and she moaned pleasurably as his mouth met hers. Then she yelped and pushed him away when his lips touched the aching bruise Kirk had left.

"What?" Murphy gasped, sitting up, his chest heaving.

Hope shook her head, unable to answer him, her eyes filling with tears.

"What did I do?"

"Hurts," she gasped, touching her mouth.

"I'm sorry," he said, grabbing for the towel on the floor and draping it around himself again.

"Not your fault."

"Yes, it is. I shouldn't have pushed you." Hugh had warned him; how could he have forgotten so quickly? He felt like a jerk.

"You didn't push me," she said, but he wasn't listening. He was heading for the door.

"I'll get dressed and go," he said.

"Wait . . ." Hope protested, trying to stand and getting her leg tangled in the sheet. He went through the door and closed it behind him. She bolted off the bed and then caught sight of herself in the dresser mirror, breasts nearly exposed, the buttons ripped from the front of her blouse so it flapped like a jacket around her. She tore it off and grabbed a robe from her closet, then dashed after him.

Murphy came out of the bathroom as she entered the hall. He was still unshaven, fully dressed in the clothes he had worn the night before. There was a rip in his shirt, his coat was rumpled and his tie dangled untied from his neck, but he was obviously ready to go.

"Dennis, please stay and listen to me," Hope began, but he brushed past her.

"I can't. I have to go," he said.

"Why do you have to go?"

"Things to do."

Hope dashed in front of the door and blocked his exit. "Will you stop being so stubborn?" she said, glaring at him.

Ironically, he had never looked more attractive to her than at this moment, when he was leaving: his damp hair was springing into waves, his excitement had brought color to his face and a smokiness to his eyes. The beard shadowing his cheeks gave him a vaguely piratical air.

"I'm not being stubborn," he replied, avoiding her eyes.

"Then what are you doing?"

"I'm going."

Hope sighed. "I wasn't rejecting you," she said gently.

"Of course you were, and you should have been. Last night you were nearly raped and twelve hours later I'm putting the same moves on you. I should be shot."

Hope stared at him. "Dennis, are you crazy? You can't compare the two events."

But he was in no mood to listen. "Call Hugh if you need any medical help. I left his number by the phone. Let us know when you feel up to coming back to work." He turned and walked out, pulling the door closed behind him.

Hope picked up a pillow from the couch and threw it at the door in frustration.

"And he just left?" Meg said in astonishment, sipping her ice tea, wide-eyed.

"Left, and I haven't seen him since. Sue called and told me to take a few days off, his brother called to see if I was all right, but from the esteemed D.A. I have not heard one word." Hope stopped talking long enough to apply lipstick gingerly to her mouth. The bruise had faded to a saffron yellow and the swelling had gone down, but the skin there was still sensitive.

"I can't figure it out," Meg said.

"You're not alone."

"I mean, only an insecure kid would react that way. You could accuse Murphy of being lots of things, but that isn't one of them."

"I wanted to make love with him, Meg. I really did. I guess I knew it all along, but to have him there with me, all but naked . . ."

"Please," Meg said throatily. "I feel weak at the thought."

"There must be something more to it."

"Maybe he's afraid of getting involved again since his wife died, and you gave him a convenient excuse to pull out of the situation."

"I think I'm in love with him."

"You decide this *now,* after complaining about him so often my eardrums are perforated?"

"Maybe I was protesting too much."

"What are you going to do?"

"I don't know. If his behavior in the past is any clue, he will probably act as if I'm a leper when I return to work."

The telephone rang and Hope answered it on the third ring. She listened for a long moment and then said, "Oh, thank you, Your Honor, I'm just fine." She mouthed "the mayor" at Meg, who made an impressed face.

Hope listened again and said, "I appreciate your concern, but I'm fine."

Meg got up and refilled her glass of ice tea.

The listening pause got longer and then Hope said, "Do you really think that will be necessary?"

Meg glanced at her, alerted by Hope's tone.

"Of course I understand," Hope said resignedly.

Meg raised her brows inquiringly, and Hope shook her head disgustedly.

"Of course I'll be in touch," Hope said. "Thank you for calling. Goodbye."

"What's going on?" Meg said as Hope replaced the receiver in its cradle.

"The mayor is disbanding his task force to investigate the D.A.'s office," Hope replied evenly.

Meg put down her glass.

"It seems word of my adventure with Mr. Kirk is making the rounds," Hope said.

"Translation—all the conservatives are up in arms that your program put a dangerous criminal back on the streets and they don't want it to happen again," Meg said.

"That's about the size of it. His Honor is calling a press conference for Monday. I'm to give a report covering the results of my investigation—312 cases reviewed, two judged to be actionable, one of which was Kirk's. On that basis, the mayor has determined that there is no justification for continuing the review process."

"Does he think that's going to fool anybody?"

"Probably not, but it will be over, and that's what he wants. God forbid I should spring another rapist."

"You were right to bring Kirk's case up for review," Meg said consolingly. "He may be the scum of the earth, but he *was* unfairly treated according to the law."

Hope nodded wearily.

"I guess you'll be going back to private practice sooner than you thought," Meg observed.

"And I won't be seeing Murphy again, either," Hope observed miserably.

"Come on, don't look like that. He won't be dead."

"I won't see him at work, will I?" Hope countered.

The doorbell rang.

"My, I'm popular today," Hope said. She answered the door and discovered Sue Chancellor on the other side of it, holding a bunch of daisies.

"I'm performing a corporal work of mercy, visiting the sick," Sue announced.

"I'm not sick."

"Well, then, I'm just visiting."

"Come on in," Hope said, stepping aside.

She introduced Sue to Meg, who said, "Nice to meet you. Hope, I have to go. I have a million things to do. I'll call you tomorrow." Meg left as Hope searched for a vase tall enough to accommodate the flowers.

"Have a seat anywhere. Would you like a glass of ice tea?"

"Sure." Sue sank onto the sofa as Hope arranged the flowers and then joined her, handing her a drink. "I assume you've heard?" Sue said.

"The mayor just called me."

"News travels fast," Sue observed.

"It sounds like he wants to sweep me under the rug as soon as possible. I assume Murphy is overjoyed."

"Not noticeably. He's been in a snit ever since your encounter with Mr. Kirk."

"Really?"

Sue nodded. "Biting everyone's head off, striding around with that bulldog look on his face. I guess it's understandable—the whole thing must have brought back memories about his wife."

Hope sat forward eagerly. "What exactly *did* happen with his wife? People have referred to it obliquely, but I've never been rude enough to ask a direct question about it."

"Until now," Sue said, grinning.

"Yes."

"Well, it's quite a story. Murphy comes from one of the worst sections of south Philadelphia—real poverty. He and his brother were orphaned after their mother died, raised by the Christian Brothers. He went to college on an athletic scholarship and on to law school on a work-study program."

"His brother is a doctor."

"No kidding. That's quite an accomplishment, considering they had no parents after they were around ten and twelve. Anyway, I guess it seemed he had finally left his former life behind when he married the daughter of a prominent wealthy businessman, some guy with a chain of retail stores, and established a well-heeled suburban practice while he was still a kid, in his twenties."

Hope listened, trying to relate all of this to the hardnosed man she knew now.

Sue sighed. "Then one night, when his pregnant wife came into town to meet him for dinner after he had a late court session, she stopped for gas at an inner city station and was killed by a couple of thugs robbing the safe there."

"Oh, my God."

"Suddenly it was all over—the marriage, the kid, everything. After that, Murphy dropped his private practice and joined the D.A.'s office as a prosecutor, working up to his present position in less than four years."

Hope was silent a long time, then said, "How do you know so much about it?"

Sue smiled sadly. "It has probably not been lost on you that I have something of a crush on the man."

Hope said nothing.

"My decision to move to New York was made largely to get away him. It's hard to carry a torch as bright as mine and be met with benign indifference in return."

Hope looked away.

"But you wouldn't know about that," Sue said.

Hope glanced at her.

"He's got the hots for you," Sue said.

Hope started to reply, then shut her mouth.

"Did you hear anything of what happened at Kirk's arraignment?" Sue asked her.

Hope shook her head.

"Murphy had to be physically restrained from attacking the defendant. He received a stern warning from the judge and a letter of censure from the bar association."

"Wonderful," Hope said flatly.

"All of which has led me to conclude that my imminent departure is timely. I will leave the field to the victor, with all best wishes." Sue stood abruptly.

"I'm not the victor, Sue. I haven't seen Murphy since Kirk's arrest. I could be in Arkansas for all he knows."

"He knows. He's had a patrol car assigned to make the rounds past your building, twice every shift. I saw the order for it myself on his desk."

"Why on earth has he done that?" Hope asked, aghast.

"Because he wants to keep tabs on you, isn't it obvious? He must think you have a boyfriend or something."

Hope remembered the date she had canceled the night of the attack. "How could he convince the police that it was necessary to watch me?" Hope asked Sue.

Sue shrugged. "He's the D.A.—he probably gave them some cock-and-bull story. You already *were* attacked, remember? Maybe his concern is legitimate—Kirk might have confederates. Who knows? The cops love Murphy. They do anything he asks."

Hope didn't know whether to be outraged or amused. The man couldn't pick up the phone or ring her doorbell, but he was having her watched by the *police.*

Sue extended her hand. "I guess I should say goodbye," she said. "It looks like you won't be coming back to the office, and I'll be gone by next week."

Hope reached out impulsively to hug her. "Thanks, Sue. You've been a good friend to me. Keep in touch."

"I will."

Hope watched her leave, then walked over to her window to peer down at the street.

It was deserted. No patrol car in sight.

She smiled to herself and dropped the curtain.

On Monday morning, Hope wore a tailored beige suit with a carnation-pink bow blouse to the press conference. She sat next to the mayor as he explained his reason for disbanding the review committee. He was relieved to learn that the situation in the D.A.'s office was not what he had feared, and so had decided that Hope would not be continuing in her position, since it appeared unnecessary.

Then Hope issued her statement, complete with copies ready to be filed, saying that the incidents of civil-rights abuse in the D.A.'s office were isolated and minor. The spirit of zealous prosecution, which could sometimes lead to instances of overkill, had not crossed the line into major curtailment of First Amendment freedoms under District Attorney Murphy.

The press listened to all of this in suspicious silence. Then they unloosed a barrage of questions relating to the Kirk incident; they had not been misled by the smoke screen. Hope kept stealing glances at Murphy's impassive face at the other end of the table as the conference continued. He had not glanced her way once, but she felt his presence as if he were only inches away from her.

"Mr. Murphy, do you regard the attack on Miss Jarvis by Robert Kirk to be a vindication of your tough stand on the incarceration of repeat offenders?" a female reporter asked.

"I regard the attack on Miss Jarvis as unfortunate. She did her duty as she saw it. Kirk's case was one of only two that she brought up for review. I think we should let the matter rest there."

The press persisted a bit longer, but it was all over after about an hour. Hope lingered until everyone had dispersed from the city-hall press room, then she left, as well.

She was surprised to find Murphy waiting for her in the deserted hallway.

"Hi," he said.

Hope merely looked at him and waited.

"I'm sorry about the way I left that morning at your apartment," he said.

Hope said nothing.

"I'd like to take you to dinner by way of apology," he offered.

"That won't be necessary," she said.

"Look, Hope, don't rake me over the coals about this. I know I have some explaining to do. I behaved badly, but I want to make up for it. We won't be seeing each other at work anymore—can't we go out and have a nice evening together?"

"I don't know. Can we?" she said archly.

"Just one night, and then if you hate it you never have to see me again. Okay?"

Hope relented. "Okay."

He smiled, and she felt her heart flip-flop in her chest.

"I'll pick you up on Friday night at eight," he said.

"Fine."

As he walked away, Hope realized that she was smiling, too.

# Six

Hope was in a fever of anticipation about her "date" with Murphy on Friday. He hadn't said where they were going, but on Thursday afternoon she returned from a conference with Greg Collins about resuming her practice to find a basket of gardenias sitting in the hall in front of her door. There was a note attached to it which read, "Dress casually. I hope you like Mexican food. Dennis."

She went inside and hung up the silk dress she had been ready to press and looked through her collection of jeans, none of which fitted her correctly. She had spent her life in search of a pair of dungarees which could adapt to her lean height, pants which didn't leave her ankles exposed to the breeze and her waist defined at her armpits. She finally selected the least offensive pair and teamed the slacks with a natural cotton sweater and gazed at herself in the mirror. Well, she was no threat to Paulina Porizkova, but for a woman whose life was completely off balance, Hope didn't look half-bad.

She didn't *want* to be in love with Murphy, but she was a realist, and she recognized that she *was*. Hope had been running away from sexual commitment her whole life, but she had been ready to sleep with Murphy that morning he came into her room. No doubts or hesitation, no quibbling with her conscience: she was ready. That told her more than all the rationalizing and deep thinking her legal training had imposed upon her. The realization was scary, but also liberating. She was ready to meet him on his own terms and take it from there.

When the doorbell rang on Friday night, Hope answered it with a calm born of a resolution to face her fate. She opened the door to see Murphy, looking uncharacteristically nervous and very tired. It was the first time she had seen him dressed in anything but a suit, and the casual clothes made him appear years younger, almost boyish. He was wearing a navy Windbreaker with a light blue polo shirt and tan chinos, his bare feet encased in leather boat shoes. He was standing with his hands in his pockets, his expression wary.

"Hi," he said.

"Hi."

"Ready to go?"

Hope nodded and they went into the hall, where she locked her door behind them.

"Where are we going?" she asked.

"For a ride. Upper Bucks."

Bucks County was adjacent to Philadelphia, and the northern portion of it was quite rural. When she didn't respond, he glanced at her and said, "Afraid to take a little trip with me?"

"Not at all. You've proven yourself trustworthy."

He stopped walking. "Is that a shot?"

Hope looked at him. "I beg your pardon?"

"Is that a reference to the way I left you the other morning?" he asked.

My, he was certainly touchy about that. "Not at all," Hope replied smoothly. "You saved me from Kirk. I think that's sufficient evidence of your good character."

He muttered something under his breath that she didn't catch, then held the car door open for her in silence.

He didn't seem in a chatty frame of mind, and Hope fell in with his mood, listening to the Gershwin score he had playing on the stereo and watching the lovely scenery go by outside the window. The spring evening was cloudy and chilly, but with plenty of color supplied by the profusion of new flowers. They drove for about forty minutes before he pulled into the parking lot of a country-style restaurant Hope had seen advertised on television.

"This okay?" he asked her.

"Sure," Hope replied.

He led the way inside and hailed the owners, a husband-and-wife team who greeted him as if he were a long-lost relative. He and Hope were given a secluded table behind a screen of standing plants.

"They seem to like you a lot," Hope said, nodding toward the smiling couple.

"Restaurateurs are always glad to see bachelors," Murphy replied shortly.

Once they were settled in their seats, he ordered two bottles of Dos Equis beer.

"They're both for me," Murphy said, as Hope opened her mouth to protest. "I have a feeling I'm going to need them. Do you want something else?"

She shook her head.

Once the waiter left, Murphy looked at Hope and said, "Are we having fun yet?"

She didn't know how to reply.

"I guess this little social occasion wasn't such a good idea," he observed tightly.

"Dennis, what's wrong?" Hope asked. "You look tense and exhausted."

He shrugged. "I was up all night, overseeing the arrest of some solid citizens, and then had an early arraignment this morning. I guess I should have canceled this evening, but—"

"But?"

"I wanted to see you," he said simply. "I suppose it was selfish. I'm not exactly scintillating company tonight." He toyed with the beer bottle, rolling its base on the tablecloth. He looked up suddenly. "You didn't have to come here with me because you're grateful to me, Hope," he said.

"That isn't why I came," she replied.

"Really, Hope? Is that the truth? Because gratitude isn't what I want."

"What do you want?"

"You," he said, looking at her with an expression that made her pulse leap wildly. "This has passed the social stage for me. I can't play nice and go on dates and make small talk. I can't think about anything else but taking you to bed, and I'm too punch drunk tonight to do anything else but admit it."

Hope gripped the edge of the table, her knuckles white, her eyes on his face.

"I left you the morning after Kirk attacked you because I was scared," Murphy continued. "When you pulled back for that split second it gave me the chance to think about what I was doing, getting involved again with a woman who might leave me—walk out, or give up on me, or die—" He stopped short. "I guess I should tell you about my wife," he concluded quietly.

"I heard something about it," Hope said gently.

He smiled humorlessly. "Everyone in town has 'heard something about' my tragic tale," he said, nodding.

The waiter brought the drinks. Murphy opened the first bottle and took a long pull before adding, "I had been married less than a year. My wife was five months pregnant. She interrupted a gas station robbery and was killed. The two perpetrators had long records—one of them had only been paroled a week earlier."

"I'm so sorry," Hope said softly.

"Thus began my current illustrious career," he added dryly. "I was going to get them all, put them all away, every scumbag and dirtball who could end the life of an innocent in a split second of mindless violence. I was also never going to repeat that loss, that pain I felt when everything was taken away from me. And then all my resolves went out the window when you turned up again."

"Again?"

"Your moot-court competition. You didn't remember me, but I remembered you."

"You never expressed any interest then, Dennis. I would have remembered that, believe me."

"When I asked around, I found out that you were engaged, so I didn't pursue you. What happened?"

"I broke it off. I realized I wasn't in love with him."

Murphy nodded, then sat back in his chair. "When I heard the mayor was sending you to my office, every self-defense mechanism I possessed jumped right into the front lines. Knowing that I was going to see you every day—well, I was spooked, I can tell you." He drained the first bottle of beer and opened the second one.

"I guess that explains my enthusiastic reception," Hope said, smiling slightly.

"Oh, I wouldn't have been happy to see anyone on that mission, but the fact that it was you—" He broke off and shook his head. "And then when you wouldn't listen to me about Kirk—" he shrugged "—it was like you were taking the same chances my wife took."

"I thought you were just protecting your office, your conviction rate, when you objected to his release," Hope said.

"I knew he would come after you."

"Please, don't remind me," Hope whispered, shuddering at the still-vivid memory.

"I feel this need to protect you, whether you want me to or not," he said, his face grave.

"Does that include the patrol cars that have been gliding past my building every couple of hours?"

"You noticed," he said sheepishly.

"Do you really think that's necessary now?"

"I just want to be on the safe side."

"The safe side of what? Kirk is in jail."

"May I take your order?" the waiter said, appearing at Murphy's shoulder.

Hope shook her head.

"Not just yet, pal. Give us some time," Murphy said.

The waiter disappeared.

"I guess it must be obvious from this discussion that I don't know how to court you," Murphy said. "I'm resorting to these high-handed—okay, ridiculous—tactics because I've forgotten what to do. It's been too long, and to tell you the truth I was never any damn good at it in the first place."

"Your wife didn't mind."

"No."

"Neither do I," Hope said, and took his hand.

He gripped her fingers tightly.

"Do you want me?" he asked, his gaze direct and searching. "Do I have a chance?"

Hope couldn't speak past the lump in her throat. She nodded, her eyes filling with tears.

"I hope the fact that you're crying is a good sign," he said, lifting her hand to his lips.

She nodded again.

"Do you want to get out of here now?" he asked, lifting her hand to his lips.

"Yes," she said, finding her voice.

"Where?" he asked.

"Aren't there rooms upstairs?" she said. "I saw a sign outside."

He gazed at her across the table, his eyes lambent. "Are you sure?" he asked.

"I'm sure."

He stood up and pulled a bill out of his wallet, dropping it on the table.

"I'll be right back," he said.

Hope waited, her stomach fluttering with butterflies, until he returned with a key in his hand.

"Let's go," he said, holding out his hand.

Hope rose and took it, her slender fingers lost in his large palm. They went to the back of the restaurant and climbed a flight of wooden stairs, which led to a carpeted hallway with several doors opening off of it on either side.

"Second on the left," he said, and unlocked the door. The room was charming, tucked under the eaves with a worn Oriental rug covering the washed floorboards and a flowered bedspread which matched the chintz curtains. There was a silver bowl of fresh flowers on a side table and a small fire glowing in the grate of a corner fireplace.

"This room looks ready for occupancy," Hope said.

"It is. We're occupying it."

Hope turned to gaze at his conspicuously innocent face. "Dennis, what did you do?"

"I booked a room. Why are you looking at me like that?"

"Did you put somebody out on the street?"

"I made a small monetary contribution to encourage the proprietors to give up this room. Okay?"

Hope walked over to the window and looked out at the parking lot, her back to him.

"If you've changed your mind, we can go. I don't want to force you into anything," he said, misinterpreting her hesitation.

"Just give me a minute in the bathroom, okay?" Hope said, stalling for time.

He nodded.

She went into the adjoining bathroom and stared at herself in the mirror, at the two high spots of color on her cheeks and the glittering, excited eyes.

Should she just come right out and tell him that she had never done this before? If she didn't say anything, he would certainly figure it out once they were making love. He was a grown man who'd been married, and he was well versed in the ways of the world. Would he laugh, think she was backward, run out the door? Virgins of her age were not exactly thick on the ground, and he obviously thought she was experienced.

The morning after Kirk attacked her, and Murphy had come into her bed, she'd been half-asleep and too glad of his presence to think much about what she was doing. But she was wide-awake and thinking clearly now, and what she thought was that he'd better know he was going to bed with a beginner.

Determined to tell him, she walked out into the bedroom and saw him sitting in the chair before the fire. As she got closer she noticed that his eyes were closed, his dark lashes fanned on his cheeks, and he was breathing evenly.

Her first impulse was to laugh. She had stayed in the bathroom so long debating the sorry state of her virginity that her potential lover had passed out cold. Thinking that this episode was typical of her stalled love life, she sighed and pulled off her sweater, then stepped out of her jeans, preparing for bed. She would let Murphy sleep in the chair; it was deep and wide and looked comfortable. She unbuttoned her blouse and draped it over the footboard, then shook back her hair and turned to pull the coverlet off the bed.

"Don't stop there," Murphy's husky voice said.

She started and looked over at him. He was watching her intently with slitted eyes.

"I thought you were asleep," she said. She could feel herself blushing.

"Never less asleep than at this moment," he said in a low tone. "Come here."

Dressed only in her bra and panties, Hope walked over to him. He held out his arms and she curled up on his lap.

"God, you feel wonderful," he muttered, his mouth against her neck. He raised his head and kissed her gently, moving his mouth lightly over hers, increasing the pressure and then drawing back until she responded avidly, clutching him and kissing him back urgently. He ran his hands up and down her bare arms, parting her lips with his tongue, then shifted her weight on his legs to draw her closer. Hope's head fell back to expose her throat as he bent to kiss her collarbone, the silken cleft between her breasts, then stroked her bare spine with his free hand as he felt for the catch of her bra.

He released it in a second. The scrap of lace fell to the floor and Murphy pressed his flushed face to her breasts in the same instant, making a guttural sound of utter gratification. His skin was on fire and his mouth was everywhere, sucking her nipples, searing her tender flesh.

Hope was on sensory overload, weak as a kitten, submitting blissfully; if he had not been holding her so tightly, she would have fallen. She opened her eyes dreamily and looked down at him, saw his tousled dark hair contrasting with her fair skin, and his mouth reddened and swollen from her kisses. She put her hand to the back of his neck and held his head against her, closing her eyes again. He drew a breath that caught in the middle, like a sigh, and burrowed deeper.

"I love you," he said against her shoulder, then raised his head to kiss her mouth. "I love you," he said again.

Then he stood and carried her to the bed.

Hope looked up at him as he laid her gently down and then stepped back, stripping off his jacket and his shirt in quick, efficient movements. When dressed he looked slim, but clothing leaned him, disguising broad shoulders and well-developed biceps. The mat of black chest hair she remembered from their embrace at her apartment narrowed to a line at his waist and disappeared below it. When he unbuckled his belt, she looked away, her heart pounding, her mouth dry. A second later the bed depressed with his weight and he pulled her against him.

He was still wearing his pants. Pushing a lock of hair back from her forehead and gazing down at her he said, "What is it?"

Hope buried her face in the crook of his arm. "I'm shy," she whispered.

He turned off the light on the stand next to the bed. "Is that better?" he said.

She nodded but didn't raise her head.

"Hope?"

She forced herself to look at him.

"Do you want me to stop?" he asked.

"No, no, I love you, too, I love you so much," she said, seizing his hand and covering it with kisses.

The gesture, and the words, reassured him and he lifted her back into his arms. "Then you'd better tell me what's going on," he said, nuzzling her.

"I've never done this before," she blurted, then tensed for his reaction.

"Done what? Slept with me? I think I would have remembered." Then the full import of what she had said sank in and he lifted her chin to look into her eyes.

"Hope, are you saying . . . ?"

She nodded miserably.

"Never?"

She shook her head.

"I'll be damned."

"Probably, and I'll still be a virgin."

"But you were engaged," Murphy said in amazement, not listening to her.

"That doesn't mean I was making love."

"If you were my fiancée, you would have been making love with me," Murphy said flatly.

"So I guess you're turned off now, right?" Hope said.

"Oh, darling, of course not," he replied, gathering her close and slipping into a prone position beside her. "This just adds something else to the equation, that's all." He stroked her hair absently, obviously thinking.

"Like what?"

"Well, for one thing, I don't want to hurt you."

"I'll survive it. Billions have."

"For another thing...well, I guess it's kind of a milestone for you, isn't it?"

"Millstone is more like it."

"I never would have guessed it," he said.

"I'm noticing something here," Hope said.

"And what is that?"

"Two minutes ago you were ripping off my underwear and now we're having a philosophical conversation."

He began to shake, and she realized he was laughing.

"I don't think it's funny," Hope said. "I shouldn't have said anything about it."

"I'm glad you told me."

"Really?"

"Yes."

"Then why are we talking?"

"Hope, I'm surprised, that's all. And feeling touched and privileged and flattered."

"That's all very nice, but you've gone from making passionate love to me to treating me like I'm a piece of Limoges porcelain. That's not what I want."

"What do you want?" he said huskily. "Tell me."

"This," she said, and returned his hand to her bare breast.

"Ah," he murmured, caressing her. "That I can do." He rubbed her nipple with his thumb until it became hard, then bent to take it in his mouth. Her eyes fluttered closed. He sucked on one breast, then the other, until Hope was turning restlessly, digging her fingers into his hair and arching her back. He moved his palm over the smooth surface of her abdomen and hooked his forefinger under the lace border of her panties. She lifted her hips and he pulled the panties off, then slid his hand between her legs and cupped her.

Hope sighed deeply, biting her lower lip, as he raised his head and kissed her throat, her chin, her cheek, all the while increasing the pressure of his caressing hand. She moaned and clutched at him as he finally kissed her mouth. She wound her arms around his neck and kissed him back ardently, marveling at the satiny feel of his bare back, the warmth of his skin. When he guided her hand to his belt she fumbled with the buckle and he drew back.

"Let me," he said, and moved off the bed to undress fully. She watched his movements, which seemed to flicker in the firelight, and when he joined her again she gasped with the shock of his totally naked body against hers.

"Easy, easy," he said softly. She relaxed gradually and then snuggled into his shoulder, feeling safe and protected within the curve of his arm.

"Can you feel how much I want you?" he murmured.

Hope moaned softly in response.

"Do you want to touch me?" he asked her.

"Yes."

He took her hand and placed it on his belly, where she could feel the ridges of muscle and, below, the dense mat of curling hair. He sucked in his breath as her exploring fingers moved lower and encircled him, her inexperienced movements inflaming him more than the touch of the most experienced courtesan might have done. When he could take no more he rolled away from her, his arm thrown across his eyes.

"Dennis?"

He lowered his arm and looked at her, his eyes heavy, very blue. Then he gestured for her to move next to him, and she did.

"I don't want to rush you," he said, when he could talk.

She propped herself on one elbow and looked down at him.

"I'm afraid I can't go slow," he added.

"Then go fast," she said, smiling at him tenderly. "I've waited too long already."

He took her at her word, reaching for her and rolling her under him, positioning her. When he caressed her again, she lifted to meet him eagerly. She was ready; she sighed luxuriously and her legs drew apart. When he poised above her, she wrapped her legs around his hips and said, "Yes, now."

He entered her slowly, and she bucked once, stiffening. He stopped immediately, waited until she arched against him, asking for more. Then he drove deeper, heard her helpless sound of submission, and knew that all would be well.

"Are you all right?" he asked her, fighting for control, resisting the urge to plunge, and plunge again.

Hope ran her hands down his sweat-slicked spine and felt the age-old pride of possession.

"I'm just fine," she murmured, and kissed his salty neck.

He took her at her word and began to move in a rhythm Hope's body recognized instinctively, and learned at once.

Hope woke to the sound of falling rain. Murphy was sleeping with his arm flung across her, and the fire had burned low. She held up her wrist but couldn't see her watch in the darkened room. She lifted his arm gingerly; he stirred but did not waken. She went over to the fireplace, and by the light of the dying flames saw that it was eleven-fifteen.

She was starving. But she doubted if there was such a thing as room service in this establishment, so she decided to take a shower. She touched the back of her hand to her lips; she hated to wash away Murphy's scent on her skin. Her well-used body was singing, but tired, with several tender places on her thighs that she was sure would turn into bruises. A hot shower with lots of lovely soap would do wonders.

When Hope emerged from the bathroom, surrounded by a cloud of steam as she opened the door, Murphy was sitting up in bed swathed in the sheet, smiling at her.

"You're awake," she said, tightening the voluminous towel around herself.

"Of course I'm awake. Who could sleep through that deafening chorus of 'Oh! Susanna' you were warbling?"

"I was not warbling," she said, dancing out of his path when he reached for her.

"Then it must have been a water buffalo in there," he said, laughing softly.

"You're making fun of me," she said, her fledgling sexual confidence not up to his teasing.

He vaulted out of bed and seized her in a bear hug. "I am not making fun of you. I'm glad you're happy. I'm happy, too."

"Are you?" she whispered, rubbing her nose against his shoulder, her eyes closed.

"How can you ask?" he countered.

"I was afraid I might have been a disappointment. I'm not very good at it yet."

"It?" he said.

She punched him lightly, and he flinched dramatically.

"You know what I mean," she said.

"You're very good at *it,* a natural if I ever met one, and you will get better all the time. I plan to give you lots of practice," he replied, nibbling her ear.

"If I don't die of starvation first," she muttered.

"What was that?" he asked, distracted by running his tongue down the side of her neck.

"Dennis, aren't you *hungry?* We had no dinner and it's almost midnight."

"I guess I've had other things on my mind." He peeled off her towel and dropped it on the floor.

"Dennis," Hope said in a strong voice. "Food."

"Nag, nag, nag." He went to the phone as Hope admired his rear view while he picked up the receiver.

"They only serve Mexican food here," he said to her as he dialed the front-desk extension listed on the phone. "Do you really want fajitas at the witching hour?"

"At this point I would be grateful for a peanut butter and jelly sandwich," Hope said, wrapping the towel around her once more.

Murphy had a brief conversation with someone on the other end of the phone, which resulted in a satisfied smile as he hung up and turned to face her.

"Leftover chili from the restaurant and sopaipillas on the way up," he said.

"What's a sopaipilla?" Hope asked.

"A sticky, high-calorie dessert. Very good for you."

"How did you get into Mexican food?" Hope asked. "It's not an enthusiasm I would associate with South Philly."

"One of the Christian Brothers in the home where I was raised was Mexican, and a great cook. Hugh and I both got addicted."

He rarely made reference to his childhood, and Hope seized the opportunity to learn more. "How long were you in the home?"

"From when I was ten and Hugh twelve." He picked his pants up from the foot of the bed and stepped into them.

"What happened to your parents?"

Murphy shrugged, zipping his fly. "My father was a bad guy, a jerk, abusive. When he finally took off for good, we were glad to see him go. But then my mother died of T.B. a couple of years later, and my relatives were worse off than we were and couldn't care for us. So we wound up in the orphanage."

"Tuberculosis? Who dies of that today?"

"Poor people, Hope," he replied, making her feel naive and ashamed. "And it wasn't today, it was twenty-five years ago."

"I'm sorry," she said, chastened. "I shouldn't have said that, I wasn't thinking."

"Don't worry about it. You had an understandable reaction. It *was* a shame—the disease is so treatable when diagnosed early. But my mother wasn't exactly running to doctors."

"How did you and your brother get an education?" Hope asked, fascinated by the story.

"The Brothers realized we were bright and they helped us get scholarships. They worship learning almost as much as they worship God, so Hugh and I wound up in the right place." He put his arm around her and kissed her hair. "Enough about my checkered past. Why are you wearing that towel again?"

There was a knock at the door.

"Cheese it, it's the cops," he whispered.

"It had better be my food," Hope said as she walked into the bathroom.

"*Your* food? Who phoned for it?"

Hope shut the bathroom door in his face. She heard the drone of the muted conversation he had with their visitor, and then he called, "Chow time."

Hope emerged to see a little wheeled cart, draped with a snowy cloth, set up next to the bed. It was laden with serving dishes which steamed when Murphy removed the lids.

"Would her ladyship like some chili?" he said as he loaded a plate with it.

Hope took her plate and a fork in reverential silence and dug in immediately, sitting on the edge of the bed.

"Why don't you weigh two hundred pounds?" he asked in amazement, watching her eat.

"I'm not usually this hungry," she said.

"Are you pregnant already?" he asked, smiling.

Hope didn't know what to say.

"It would be nice if you are, because I think we should get married as soon as possible," he said.

Hope dropped her fork to her plate.

"Don't you agree?" he asked.

Hope swallowed noisily.

"This is not the ecstatic response I was anticipating," he observed, breaking a roll in half.

"I'm just ... surprised," she said.

"Why? I love you, you love me, we just shared a highly satisfactory sexual encounter and we're both of legal age. Why should you be surprised?"

"I just am," she said lamely.

He gestured expansively. "I realize that some romantics might say that receiving a marriage proposal while wolfing a bowl of chili con carne is not the most lyrical of scenarios, but—"

"I was not wolfing," Hope replied, and put the plate down on the cart abruptly.

"Well, what do you have to say?" he asked.

Hope shook her head, looking away from him.

He sat next to her. "What's wrong?"

She slumped onto his shoulder.

"Are you crying again?" he asked.

She nodded.

He sighed. "Hope, this is not the way this is supposed to go. When I ask you to marry me, you're supposed to scream with unrestrained joy and throw yourself into my arms."

"I'm joyful," she sobbed. "I'm very joyful."

"It doesn't sound like it."

She reached up and hooked her arms around his neck, kissing him eagerly.

"Now, that's more like it," Murphy said against her mouth, and pushed her back onto the bed.

"Aren't you hungry?" Hope asked as he dropped her towel over the side of the bed.

"Not for food," he replied, and proved it.

# Seven

In the morning Hope woke to find that Murphy was gone and a note was pinned to the pillow next to her head.

*"Gone to get breakfast. Back soon. D."*

Hope rolled over indolently and gazed at the ceiling through slitted eyes. She had never felt better in her life. She was, of course, exhausted, having slept very little, spending most of the night in strenuous activity. Nevertheless her sense of well-being was overwhelming, and she stretched luxuriously, as preening and self-satisfied as a cat.

So that was sex. Well, she would have much more of it, and as soon as possible. She felt renewed and reborn, but at the same time so lonely she could hardly believe it. She longed for Murphy intensely; his absence, however brief, was a physical pain. She had never understood what love was, how it could control lives, why people behaved as they did when caught in its throes.

Now she knew.

Hope was just stepping reluctantly into her wrinkled jeans when Murphy came through the door with a paper bag in his hands.

"Oh, no, you're all dressed," he said, disappointed. "I'll just have to remedy that." He set the bag down and turned toward her.

Hope ran to him and threw her arms around his neck.

"I missed you," she said, burying her face against his chest luxuriously.

"I was gone twenty minutes," he said, laughing as he gathered her into his arms.

"It was too long."

"Well, I'll just have to take off again if I'm guaranteed this kind of reception when I get back." He lifted her hair off her collar and kissed the side of her neck.

"Don't you dare." She raised her head and peered at the bag sitting on the bed. "What's in there?"

"Coffee and blueberry muffins."

Hope struggled out of his grasp. "Yum," she said, and ripped open the bag.

"I thought you might like that," he said dryly.

"Don't they serve breakfast in this place?" Hope asked, her mouth full of muffin.

"The restaurant, such as it is, doesn't open until eleven-thirty. That's from the sandwich shop down the street."

"I wish I had something clean to wear," she lamented, looking down at her rumpled sweater.

"We'll go straight back to your place so you can change."

"But everyone is going to know when they see us come downstairs in the same clothes."

"Know what?"

"What we've been doing up here."

"I think they already could have guessed that we haven't been playing backgammon. And 'everyone' consists of the couple who own this place, who I think are still asleep, and the guy down in the lobby sweeping the floor." He popped the plastic top from his cup and took a long swallow of his coffee.

"It's the principle of the thing. I'm not the type of person who sneaks off for a clandestine rendezvous and then reappears the next morning identically dressed."

"What type of person are you?" he asked, grinning at her as he put his cup down.

"I'm a reserved type of person," she said.

"Reserved?" he replied, removing the half-eaten muffin from her hand and putting it on the nightstand next to his coffee. Then he pulled her sweater over her head.

"Yes."

"Dignified?" he asked, unbuttoning her blouse.

"Certainly," she said, swallowing.

"Full of stern principles and moral rectitude?" He pulled her blouse off her arms and threw it on the floor.

"Exactly," she replied as he unhooked her bra.

"I'm so glad," he murmured. The bra joined the pile of clothes on the rug and he bent to take her nipple in his mouth. Hope closed her eyes and relaxed into the curve of his arm. His hold tightened immediately, and he reached for the buckle of his belt.

"Let me," she said, straightening, and they undressed each other with frantic haste, finally falling on the rumpled bed in a tangle of limbs. Murphy just held her for a moment, fondling her as if she were a treasured, breakable object, and then his caresses grew more intense as he pressed her back on the bed and kissed her deeply.

"When do we have to be out of here?" she asked urgently, turning restlessly beneath him, tugging him into place above her.

"Eleven," he muttered, lifting up on his elbows to look down into her face.

"Do we have time?" she asked, then moaned as he ran his hand between her legs. She arched against him urgently.

"We'll make the time," he said. He raised up to enter her and she clung to him tightly, marveling again at the softness of his skin and hair, inhaling the thrilling masculine smell of him, more intoxicating than any perfume.

"Oh, harder," she whimpered, digging her fingernails into his shoulders.

"You're a quick study," he muttered breathlessly, pinning her wrists to the bed.

"Just do it," she gasped, and he obeyed.

When they got back to Hope's apartment late that day, there were four messages on Hope's answering machine from her mother.

"I knew I should have called her," Hope muttered, sighing and dropping her handbag on the sofa.

"It's not as though you disappeared for a week," Murphy said, putting a paper bag of groceries on the counter.

"You don't know my mother. She still thinks I should get a hall pass when I go to the bathroom."

"Then you'd better break the news to her right now, give her time to adjust to it."

"What news?"

"The news that we're getting married."

Hope said nothing, hitting the button to rewind the tape on her machine.

"Well?" he said, confronting her.

Hope looked at him.

"Aren't we?" he pressed her.

"Dennis, you have to understand . . ."

"I do understand. Your mother is difficult. I'll talk to her, I'll win her over. I'm great with mothers, you'll see."

Hope shook her head helplessly. It was impossible to explain her mother to someone who had not met her; she just hoped his confidence was not misplaced. It would be unkind to convey to him that he was not exactly her mother's picture of the ideal son-in-law, harder still to explain to him that Hope felt responsible for her aging, infirm, difficult, sadly alone and isolated parent.

"You act like you're afraid of her," he said chidingly.

"Not afraid, Dennis—worried. Worried about her. She has no life but me."

"That's her fault."

Hope looked at him. "I'm aware of that, but it doesn't make the situation any easier."

"Hope, if I can deal with several hundred hardened criminals a year, I can handle your mother. I got through to you, didn't I?"

"Are you putting me in the same category with your oddball assortment of felons?" Hope asked archly.

He draped his arm around her shoulders. "Well, you were a bit of a tough sell."

"Only because you were acting like I was Joe McCarthy, investigating your office."

He kissed the tip of her nose. "Time-out, Counselor. We're in love, remember?"

The doorbell rang.

"Let's pray it's not your mother," he said in a stage whisper, his eyes widening in mock terror.

"Very funny." Hope went to the door and pulled it open to reveal Meg, attired in sweatpants and holding a canvas bag from which protruded a large bottle of Evian water.

"Hi," she said, and then her eyes traveled past Hope to Dennis, who was standing in the corner of the living room, watching her.

"I, uh, take it that you forgot we were supposed to go running," Meg said to Hope.

Hope stared at her.

"Something came up, huh?" Meg said lightly.

"Meg, I'm so sorry. It just went out of my head completely." Hope could feel herself turning red.

"I can imagine," Meg murmured, shouldering her bag. "Well, another time. I'll call you." She turned to walk off down the hall.

Hope shut the door and bolted after her.

"Meg, wait."

Meg stopped and waited for her.

"Meg, don't go. I feel like an idiot," Hope said, drawing even with her friend.

"You look wonderful," Meg replied. "What happened?"

"We spent the night together last night."

"Gee, I never would have guessed," Meg said dryly. "I meant, what happened to bring about that momentous event?"

"Dennis took me for a drive to Bucks County and then just blurted out how he felt."

"Gutsy, isn't he?"

"It's a good thing, too, because I don't think I ever would have said a thing."

"You would have, eventually. I knew you were in love with him. You were never that way with Todd."

"What way?"

"Feverish."

Hope laughed.

"Go on, Hope. Go back to him," Meg said. "Get in touch when you have the chance."

Hope embraced her friend and kissed her cheek. "Thanks for being so understanding," she said.

"Of course I understand. I should be so lucky. He's adorable. Those eyes, that gorgeous hair. Does he know that women would kill for that hair?"

Hope grinned. "I'll tell him."

Meg waved and punched the button for the elevator. "Have fun," she said.

When Hope returned, Murphy was on the phone. He gestured for her to be silent and then said, "Okay. I'll check in tomorrow." He hung up the phone, his expression concerned.

"What is it?" Hope said.

He looked at her and his face cleared. "Oh, nothing. Some reporter has been calling my office. It's probably about Kirk—I'll deal with it later." He hooked his arm around her waist and bent to kiss the hollow of her throat. "I made reservations at the Riviera Club while you were gone," he said against her neck.

"Dennis, that's so expensive!"

"So what? This is a celebration."

"What are we celebrating? My loss of virginity?"

"Among other things," he replied.

"My sexual prowess," she said teasingly.

"That, too." He glanced at his watch over her shoulder. "You'd better hustle and get ready. We have to stop at my place on the way. Unless you want me to go to dinner dressed like this."

"Oh, good. I'd like to see where you live."

"Don't get too excited. It looks like a two-star hotel in a third-world country."

"Why?" Hope asked, laughing.

"I'm never there. Getting it fixed up was always too much trouble, I guess."

"What's the decor?"

"Minimalist."

"Meaning no furniture?"

"That's about the size of it."

"But there's a bed right? There must be a bed."

"There's a bed."

"That's all we need," Hope said, and slipped her hand in between the buttons on his shirt to caress his chest lingeringly.

"We can be a little late," he said, and picked her up, carrying her into the bedroom.

\* \* \*

In the end, they were an hour late, but there were some perks associated with being district attorney, and the extreme tolerance of high-profile restaurants was one of them. When they were seated at a very good table, Murphy looked around inquiringly at their fellow diners and said, "Whose idea was it to come here, anyway? Everybody looks embalmed."

"It was your idea, Dennis."

"I was afraid of that. Look, there's a dance club on the second floor. Do you want to go up?"

"Aren't we a little overdressed?" Hope asked.

"If it's still the same as the last time I was there, everybody will be too bombed to notice. Come on."

Murphy said something to the maître d' as they passed him and handed him a bill.

"What did you tell him?" Hope asked as they ascended the wooden stairs to the second floor.

"I told him you needed madder music and stronger wine," Murphy said, taking her by the hand and running up the stairs.

"Thanks a lot."

They entered the club under a draped banner which read Forties Night. A huge rotating ball in the center of the room spangled the walls with watery streams of light, and couples glided under it to the strains of "Genesee."

There was nobody in the room under sixty.

"This is madder music?" Hope asked.

"It's a time warp," Murphy replied, laughing. "I can't believe it. The last time I was here it was Sixties Night and they were playing Martha and the Vandellas."

"Let's get out of this building before somebody offers us a senior citizens' discount."

"How about a couple of hamburgers on the way back to my place?" he asked wearily.

"Sounds great."

Forty minutes later they arrived at Murphy's apartment with a bag of fast food and a low tolerance for big-band music.

"I'll never be able to watch another World War II movie," Hope said, sighing as she kicked off her high heels and sat, looking around the living room. The place, which she had seen earlier, was not as bad as Murphy had said; it was an eclectic mixture of things left over from his marriage—a Kirman rug and a Chippendale sofa, two Eames chairs—thrown together with more recent additions acquired without regard to taste or style. Brick and two-by-four bookshelves, the type a college student might construct, took up an entire wall loaded with legal tomes and other works, and a Nautilus home gym stood in a corner next to an elaborate silk ficus tree, a relic of the earlier era. The windows had blinds without curtains, creating a sterile, hospital waiting room effect, and the walls were covered with maps and charts, not paintings or photographs. The apartment looked utilitarian rather than homey, and it made Hope want to put her arms around Murphy and hug him.

"It was a shame to waste that dress on Monty's Burger Bin," Murphy said, handing her a sandwich and a drink.

"It wasn't wasted if you saw it," Hope replied philosophically, taking a bite.

"I'd rather see it off than on," he observed, grinning as he unwrapped his burger.

Hope rattled the ice cubes in her glass. "I noticed earlier that there aren't any pictures of your wife here," she said cautiously.

"They're all in a trunk in my closet," he replied.

"Why?"

He shrugged. "Hurt too much to look at them, I guess," he said, chewing.

"Was she pretty?"

"I thought so. Not as pretty as you, in a conventional sense. But she had a glow..." He stopped.

"I'm sorry. I shouldn't have asked you to talk about her." Hope put her burger down on the coffee table.

He shook his head. "It's all right. I couldn't have fallen in love with you if I weren't over all of that. But the unfairness of it still sticks in my craw."

"Of course it does—her death was a tragedy. How could you feel any other way?"

Murphy sat next to her on the sofa and put his arm around her. "I feel like I'm getting a second chance with you."

Hope sat back with her head on his shoulder. "Do you ever compare me to her? In your mind, I mean."

He shook his head. "It's like two different lives. I can't even relate one to the other." He picked her sandwich up and handed it to her. "Now, come on. Eat up and don't worry about it."

They finished their meal and went to bed, where they seemed to be spending so much of their time. When Hope woke again, it was three o'clock a.m., and the space next to her was empty. She rose and slipped into Murphy's shirt, which fitted her like a bathrobe, and wandered out of the bedroom, rolling up the sleeves.

Murphy was sitting in the dark, wearing only a pair of jeans, staring out the window. Hope could barely see him by the small light over the kitchen stove, but the fact that he was studying the view of a brick wall next door signaled to her that something was wrong.

"What are you doing out here?" she said.

He jumped, then shook his head slightly, as if she had disturbed a profound reverie.

"You startled me," he said softly, turning and reaching out an arm to her.

"Well, who did you think it was? Last time I looked I was the only other person in this apartment."

"I thought you were sleeping," he said, tucking her into the curve of his body.

"I was until a few minutes ago," she replied. "Your absence woke me." She brushed his hair back from his forehead. "Dennis, what's wrong?"

He sighed heavily and looked away from her.

"I think you'd better tell me, otherwise I won't be able to stand the suspense."

He turned to face her. "I want you to change your area of practice," he said flatly.

Hope stared at him. "What?"

"You heard me. I want you to switch to something safer—domestic relations, real estate, corporation law, anything. Something that won't keep you in constant contact with criminals."

"Look who's talking," Hope said, stunned. She didn't know what she had been expecting, but it wasn't this.

"It's different for me," he said.

"Why? Because you're a man?"

"Let's put it this way, Robert Kirk wouldn't have been stalking me."

"That's the most ridiculous thing I've ever heard! He could have come after you with a gun, Dennis. Are you trying to tell me that never happens?"

"A woman is more vulnerable," he said stubbornly.

"Dennis, you're asking me to give up everything I've worked for since I left school! I can't start doing real estate closings or divorce settlements. I don't know the first thing about them."

"You can take a refresher course, read up on it. Other people do it all the time."

Hope surveyed him in the faint light, trying to read his face. "Does this have anything to do with Claire?" she asked.

He didn't answer, but his silence was eloquent.

"I knew I shouldn't have brought up the subject of your first marriage," Hope said quietly.

"You didn't have to bring it up, Hope. I've been thinking about it all along. Did you really think I could forget it when I saw you in the same kind of danger that killed Claire? You're a young, beautiful woman, and continuing a First Amendment practice will bring you into contact with an endless succession of Robert Kirks. The only thing strange about the episode with him is that something similar hadn't happened to you earlier."

"Are you making this a condition of our future relationship?" she said tightly.

He didn't answer.

"I think you should know by now that I don't take orders very well," she added.

"All right, all right. Will you at least think about it?"

She sighed. "I can't promise anything."

"Just think about it," he repeated. "I can't lose you the way I lost Claire, not when we can do something to prevent it." He pulled her close to him and nuzzled her neck.

"I'll think about it," she said quietly.

"I haven't cared for anyone in so long, I just want to overwhelm you with protection," he murmured. He snaked his tongue into the gap between two of the buttons on her shirt, licking her skin.

Hope closed her eyes. She had to be strong; in this situation she might promise him anything.

Murphy lowered his head and put his mouth on her breast, his lips searing her flesh through the cloth. His hands slipped up under the shirt, caressing, then he picked her up and lay her back on the couch, unbuttoning the shirt with trembling fingers. He kissed the valley between her breasts as he removed his shirt and tossed it over the back of the sofa. When he moved to sit up, she tried to hold him, but he slipped out of her grasp and stood to unzip his jeans and step out of them, kicking them aside. When he joined her again she wound her arms around his neck and sighed with satisfaction.

Hope felt him, ready, against her, and he grunted when she shifted her weight to accommodate him. Her thighs loosened and he entered her, gasping with the sensation as she turned her head away to hide her own pleasure.

"No," he said, barely able to see her expression in the darkened room. "Look at me."

Hope obeyed him, moving her eyes back to his, and what she saw there made her very sure that she would never be able to deny him anything.

They woke in the morning entwined on the couch. Hope's eyes opened when Murphy's stirring almost tumbled her to the floor.

"Sorry," he said, standing up and stretching. "I don't think I can walk. Can you tell me why we wound up here when there's a perfectly good bed in the next room?"

"You know why," Hope said, sitting up and pushing back her disordered hair.

"Yes, well, I'm getting too old for sudden bursts of lust," he grumbled, bending over to fetch his jeans and groaning as he put them on gingerly.

"I'll remember that the next time you have one," Hope said dryly, and he laughed.

He went to the cabinet over the stove, extracted a jumbo jar of freeze-dried instant coffee and turned the hot-water tap on full force in the sink.

"Do you mind telling me what you're doing?" Hope asked in a strong voice.

"Making coffee," he said, spooning the dark brown crystals into two mugs and then holding each one under the tap, which was now gushing steaming water.

"Gah," Hope said.

"Very efficient," he replied.

"Don't you have a coffeemaker?"

"Would I be doing this if I had a coffeemaker?" he inquired logically, lifting one eyebrow.

"I'll buy you one," Hope offered magnanimously, thinking of all the future mornings she would be witnessing this highly dubious procedure.

"They take too long." He came over to her and handed her the cup of muddy brew, which looked like the Mississippi at low tide and smelled worse.

"Cream?" she inquired faintly.

"I've got those flakes. Somewhere." He looked back at the kitchen doubtfully.

"Forget it." She took a sip and discovered that it wasn't too bad—if you liked discolored dishwater.

"I'm sorry if the accommodations don't meet with her ladyship's approval," he said, smiling.

"Dennis, you've barely scratched the surface of civilization here," Hope replied.

"Why should I bother? I just have this to wake me up and then I get the real thing from the corner deli on the way to the office. It works out fine."

"If you have the taste buds of an iguana," Hope observed, putting the cup aside.

"Now I'm crushed," he said, sitting next to her and sipping from his mug.

"You look it. If this coffee is a sample of Murphy's home cuisine, I guess we'll be going out for breakfast."

"Not at all. You underestimate me. I have eggs, and butter, and a loaf of bread. Scrambled eggs and toast, coming up." He stood and then hesitated. "The bread may be a little moldy, but we can cut off the corners."

Hope closed her eyes.

"And the toaster is a bit quirky—it burns everything. You have to kind of stand next to it and snatch the slices out when they start to smoke."

"Dennis," Hope said, in a martyred tone.

"Yes, dear?"

"I'd like very much to go to the Copper Kettle for breakfast, if you don't mind."

"Are you suggesting that my effort might not be nutritious and delicious?" he asked, hurt.

"Let's say I'd rather not take chances where my health is concerned," Hope replied.

"Boy, are you turning out to be a little old lady. No fun at all." He drained his cup of the foul brew.

"That's not what you said last night."

"Last night I was not myself. I was under the spell of an exotic siren who lured me to destruction with her sensual charms."

"Oh, I see." She paused for a long moment. "You said some other things last night."

His expression changed. "Yeah?" he replied cautiously.

"We have to talk some more about that," Hope said.

"Not before I've eaten. Can't it wait until later?"

"All right. You're the one who first brought up the subject," Hope reminded him.

The telephone rang.

"I wonder who wants me at this hour on Sunday morning," Murphy said.

"It can't be good news," Hope replied darkly.

Murphy answered the phone curtly, said, "Yeah?" once a few seconds later and listened in silence for what seemed like an eternity. Then he said, "Thanks for letting me know," and hung up abruptly, his expression glacial.

"What is it?"

Murphy stared at her, and it was as if he had never seen her before that moment. She was looking at a different man, not the one who had gone to answer the phone.

"That was Sue Chancellor," Murphy replied in a deadly, atonal voice. "She thought she would give me a little tip, her parting gift to me, as it were. You know that reporter who's been trying to get through to me, the one I've been ignoring? Well, he knows Sue, and when he couldn't get me, he called her in desperation."

Hope nodded, her heart beginning to pound. She had never seen him look like this, not even when he was most angry with her.

"A year ago I had another case, defendant named Harker, which was severed from the Cansino case at trial," he went on. "You remember Cansino, the occasion of your great triumph for the Constitution and all the criminal lowlifes who profit from it?"

His biting sarcasm told her this was very bad, and her mind was racing to figure it out. She vaguely remembered that Cansino had been conjoined with another case initially, but by the time it came to her the two cases were separate.

"It seems that evidence has come to light, through a convenient leak, that one of my junior assistant district attorneys, looking to make a name for himself, conspired to suppress evidence that would have exonerated Harker. It was more important to the assistant to get the conviction and show the effectiveness of my office than to follow the rules. An unfortunate attitude, to be sure, one I've previously encountered and tried to discourage.''

Hope waited, sure there was more.

"Now, someone had to comb through files and spend some time digging to come up with this—it wouldn't have been apparent to the casual observer and it certainly bypassed everybody at the trial. Now, who do we know that's very familiar with the Cansino case, has spent lots of time reviewing my back files and is very ambitious to boot? Someone who'd like to make a name by exposing a scandal at the D.A.'s office, especially someone who didn't exactly turn up rampant corruption when assigned by the mayor to look for it? A person who now needs a bone to throw to the press to show that the much-vaunted investigation wasn't a total waste of time and the taxpayers' money? Oh, and let's not forget—someone who's been, uh, *ingratiating* herself with the boss, stringing him along with kind words and kisses until the master plan can be revealed?''

Hope stared at him, her mouth dry, unable to form a reply. The accusation was so outrageous, so overwhelmingly unfair, that all she could finally manage was "Dennis, it wasn't me.''

"So you're going to sit there with your bare face hanging out and tell me you had nothing to do with this?'' he demanded furiously.

# Eight

"**O**f course I'm telling you I had nothing to do with it," Hope said starchily, recovering slightly. "How dare you accuse me of such a thing!"

"How dare I accuse you? Who else could have done it?" he shot back, hands on hips, his lips white.

"I don't know, Dennis, you've been so busy making hundreds of friends in your job for the past several years, I think it could have been just about anybody," Hope replied sarcastically, near tears but unwilling to let him see it.

"Anybody with the time and interest to pore over the case and extract every detail," he said through gritted teeth.

Hope couldn't believe this was happening. How could this man who had professed to love her turn on her so completely, in the blink of an eye?

"Dennis, I didn't do it. At this point in our relationship you should be able to take my word for that."

"Relationship?" he said, with a snort of derisive laughter. "Is that what we've been having? I've never felt so duped and deluded in my life. How you must have been grinning inwardly at my panting proposals of marriage! All that horse manure about your mother—what a stalling tactic! Because all the while you were hatching this little scheme. Must keep me on the tether until the dramatic revelation, right?"

Hope stared at him stonily, letting him rave.

"Change your practice for me?" he went on, grinning nastily. "No wonder you objected, you must have been splitting a gut laughing. Not ambitious Miss Jarvis, who wants to get her name in the paper. She's not going to dive into obscurity doing wills and property settlements—only the high-profile stuff for her. The mayor's little overseeing job didn't have exactly the effect you were anticipating, did it? But just imagine the mileage you could get out of *true*, headline-making corruption in the D.A.'s office. Ten-inch banner headlines, clients lining up at the door, you'll be on *Face the Nation* the next time we turn on the TV." His tight smile was withering.

"There's a huge flaw in your theory, Dennis. How am I going to be covered with glory when I haven't even taken credit for this wonderful scoop?"

"I just found out about it a little earlier than you had anticipated. I imagine you were going to step forward at the modestly appropriate time and reveal yourself as the person who uncovered this travesty of justice." He folded his arms, his outlined biceps and bare torso still alluring to her despite the circumstances.

"Dennis, you've gone crazy, and I'm leaving," Hope said, tearing her eyes away from him. She stood and looked around for her clothes, then remembered they were in the bedroom. Stark naked and on the verge of hysteria, she stalked with as much dignity as possible into the other room and began to dress.

Murphy followed her to the doorway and said, "When I think of all the long hours you put in at that computer, poring over those files... I was so impressed with your integrity, your dedication. Little did I know that you were plotting my destruction with every line you read."

"If that did happen with Harker, you should be glad someone uncovered it," Hope said. "Instead of berating me you should be straightening out the staff at the office and getting your own house in order."

"Don't tell me how to run my office!" he yelled. "When I need advice from a conniving, deceitful back-stabber like you I'll ask for it!"

Hope picked up her shoe and threw it at him wildly. He ducked, and it missed his head by a few inches, knocking an ABA plaque off the wall.

"That was very mature," he said, straightening.

"Well, you seemed to be regressing and so I thought I'd join you," Hope answered, grabbing her purse and bending to retrieve the shoe, which she stuck under her arm.

"Where are you going?" he demanded.

"Home," she said, charging past him unevenly.

"You came here in my car."

"Then I'll take a bus."

"It's Sunday morning."

"Then I'll walk!"

"It's at least five miles, Hope."

"What—all of a sudden you're concerned about me?" she fired at him, yanking on the outer door of the apartment, which for some reason refused to budge. She kicked it with her shod foot.

"I'll drive you home," he said grimly, watching her performance without expression.

"What is this—'I must be a gentleman regardless of the circumstances'? Forget it, buddy, 'gentleman' went out the window about ten minutes ago," she said, almost amused by his contradictory behavior. "You've spent the last quarter hour hurling accusations at me and now you want to drive me home? Go to hell." She gave a mighty shove and the door yielded, tumbling her into the hall.

He dashed after her, watching as she ran down the corridor and, ignoring the elevator, pushed open the door for the stairs.

Then he leaned back against the wall and closed his eyes. He remained in that position for several minutes, until a door opened farther down the hall and another tenant strolled by him, a green plastic bag of garbage in her hand. It wasn't until she stared at him that he remembered he wasn't wearing a shirt and went wearily back to his own apartment.

Hope walked down to the deli where Murphy bought his morning coffee and, crying quietly, made her way to the old-fashioned phone booth at the back of it. A group of Sunday munchers crowded around the glass cases, placing their orders and buying their papers. Hope pushed her way through them, praying that Meg, who was a heavy sleeper, would hear the phone ring through her weekend fog. She dialed and waited, deciding that she would take her chances on calling a cab if Meg didn't respond.

Meg answered on the fifth ring, sounding groggy and disoriented, her voice hoarse with sleep.

"Meg, it's me," Hope said.

"Hope?" Meg rasped.

"Yeah."

There was a short pause. Then, "What happened?"

"We had a fight."

"I see."

"Look, I'll tell you all about it later, but right now I need for you to come and get me. I was at Murphy's place without my car and I just picked up and walked out of there. Wearing one shoe."

Meg coughed and said, "Where are you?"

"I'm at the Rittenhouse Deli on the corner of Walnut and Rittenhouse Square."

"I know it. I'll be there in twenty minutes."

"Thanks a lot. You're a lifesaver."

Hope hung up and then waited in line for a cup of coffee, her eyes filling occasionally, drawing curious glances from some of the other patrons. Then she stood just inside the door, sipping listlessly until she saw Meg's little red car come around the corner.

Meg glided to a stop next to her and Hope climbed into the car awkwardly, balancing her coffee.

"How are you doing?" Meg asked.

"Awful."

"What the hell happened?"

"Armageddon." Hope put her back against the seat rest and closed her eyes.

"I think you'd better tell me."

Hope recounted the story briefly on the way back to her apartment, and then the two women fell silent as Meg parked the car and followed Hope up to her place.

"So I guess this will be breaking in the papers very soon," Meg finally said, as Hope unlocked her door.

"Oh, who cares?" Hope replied in a tired voice, dropping her keys on the coffee table and flinging herself on the couch.

"Murphy will care. This whole thing is going to make him look very bad."

"Good!" Hope said vindictively, and bit her lip to prevent the tears from flowing again.

"Try to give him a break, Hope. Mistrust is an occupational hazard in his job."

"Not mistrust of me. I should fall into a different category from the people he's always trying to put behind bars."

"I only meant that he is accustomed to viewing everything with a jaundiced eye."

"Meg, if you even attempt to defend him I am going to jump up and hit you," Hope said testily.

Meg sat across from Hope in an armchair and crossed her legs at the ankle. "I'm not defending him."

"Then what are you doing?"

"Trying to understand him. Didn't you tell me on the way over here that when you first started to get close, after Kirk attacked you, Murphy pulled back and later confessed that he was afraid of getting involved with you?"

"So what?"

"And then he asked you to change your practice, right, to avoid the dangers of dealing with the Kirks of the world."

"Yeah, so?"

"And you said no."

"Well, I gave him an argument."

"And I assume you think that these two events are unrelated?" Meg asked.

Hope turned her head to look at Meg disgustedly. "Meg, I'm far too upset for a Zen discussion this morning. What exactly are you getting at?"

"He's running scared because you wouldn't promise him to retire into real estate. This flap about his office scandal is just an excuse to pull away from you.''

''Meg, good thing you're not a psychiatrist, because you're wrong. He really believes that I was using him to get information to expose corruption in his office and make some hay for myself. You should have seen his face.''

''He believes it at this moment. When he calms down he'll realize what his real motivation was and call you. He's not stupid.''

''Hah! You couldn't prove it by me.''

''Maybe you should call him.''

''I'd rather eat nails.''

''You'll feel better in a few days.''

''No, I won't. He didn't give me the benefit of the doubt for one second. He got the phone call and *wham,* I was guilty. The worst felon in the court system gets more of a break from him than I did.''

''He isn't in love with the felons in the court system. He feels betrayed.''

''*He* feels betrayed! That's rich. You don't know just how rich that is, Meg.''

''You're feeling sorry for yourself.''

''Yes, I am. And if you don't want to see me doing it, then you can just go home.'' Hope turned her head away and began to cry again, silently.

''I'm not going home,'' Meg said, sighing. ''But this wallowing in misery isn't going to help you.''

''It just happened this morning. Can't I wallow for a little while, at least?'' Hope said, sniffling.

Meg suppressed a smile.

"Maybe he'll realize how wrong he is when I don't jump up to take credit for unmasking the scandal," Hope grumbled.

"I don't think that will make a difference. Even if you don't take credit for it publicly, he will think that the Mayor or whoever else you want to know about it will be privy to the information."

Hope shot her a black look. "You're a great comfort."

Meg shrugged. "I think like a lawyer."

"That's an insult to all of us."

Meg stood. "What you need is some breakfast."

Hope made a gagging sound.

"Well, *I'm* hungry, if you're not." Meg got up and went into the kitchen, and Hope put the sofa pillow over her head.

Monday morning's newspapers carried the full story, and it was all over the television later the same day. For the rest of the week the media reported Murphy's denials of wrongdoing, but his political enemies were crying foul.

They maintained that if he didn't know of the evidence suppression directly, he was responsible through chain of command and, more subtly, for creating an atmosphere of getting a conviction at any cost.

Murphy was taking a lot of heat indeed, and Hope watched him on the news and read his words in the papers, remembering his touch, his smell, the sound of his breathing in her ear when they made love. She couldn't relate those memories to the person she saw on television.

It was like their affair had happened to somebody else.

Hope's name was never mentioned in the media discussions of the scandal. The source of the story was always listed as a mystery, but Hope did not hear from Murphy, so she was sure that he continued to believe she was the leak. She did get a call from the mayor, who had come to the same conclusion as Murphy, but Hope assured His Honor she had nothing to do with the story.

Unlike Murphy, he believed her.

After several weeks went by, Hope realized that nothing was going to change. Murphy had dismissed her from his life as if she were an employee he had fired, and she knew that she had to adjust to the loss.

When the Memorial Day weekend approached, she decided to go with Meg to visit Meg's sister in Arizona. The alternatives were to stay with her mother on Long Island, or stay by herself in her apartment and brood on Murphy's perfidy. She was happy to avoid both fates by accepting Meg's invitation.

She and Meg took a flight out late Friday afternoon, and Hope was glad to put her troubles aside for a few days and enjoy the company of friends.

That same evening, Murphy was working late. There was no holiday celebration for him to look forward to, and he had a lot of work resulting from the reemergence of the Harker case. For one thing,

Harker's lawyer was demanding a retrial. For another, there had been a major drug arrest the week before and he was preparing the indictments against all three defendants. But he found it hard to concentrate. He finally sat back in his chair wearily, shoving his files aside, and rubbed his eyes.

He wished Hope would vanish from his dreams, from his thoughts, but she haunted him like a phantom. He recalled his blowup vividly, wincing at the memory. At the time it happened, he believed she had betrayed him, but since then he had calmed down and been able to see the whole scenario more rationally. Loneliness fed into his recovering stability; when Hope was around him, he found it difficult to think objectively, but her absence had made him pull back and examine the situation from a distance.

It was true that she was ambitious, but so was he. Ambition was generally thought to be an attribute, and he hoped that he wasn't such a chauvinist that he would decry in a woman what he admired in a man. And Hope's whole history bespoke a person who was honest and fair. She had never done anything unscrupulous before. Why would she jeopardize their relationship by revealing wrongdoing in his office, even if she *had* learned about it through her research? He knew her personality, her sense of justice; she would have come to him and discussed it, then together they would have decided what to do.

She was in good standing with the mayor—she was going back to her practice with accolades for a job well-done. She didn't have to turn on Murphy to further her career. With the cool head of hindsight, he now knew that what had really upset him was her refusal to abandon her First Amendment practice. He simply could not face the idea of living with Hope and worrying every day that she might suffer the same fate as his wife.

Murphy stood abruptly and began to pace his office. He had been trying to work up the nerve to call her for over a week, but the thought of her telling him to get lost forever kept him from picking up the phone. He already felt stupid and immature—adding despair to the mixture held very little appeal. But he also missed Hope terribly. He wished the whole Harker thing had never happened and found that no other woman held the slightest bit of attraction for him.

If this kept up, he might as well join the priesthood.

There was a knock at his door, and, surprised that anyone was still around, he called, "Come in."

The door opened and Dave Clendon entered, looking uncharacteristically nervous.

"Hi, Dave. I didn't know anybody was still here. The place cleared out early for the weekend."

"I came back because I need to talk to you."

"Have a seat."

Dave sat in the visitor's chair across from Murphy's desk, obviously uncomfortable. He was actually sweating.

"What's up?" Murphy said.

Dave cleared his throat. "Uh . . . this is difficult."

"Then just spit it out."

"I know who leaked the Harker story to the press."

Murphy sat up straight, afraid to speak, his attention riveted on Dave's face.

"Chloe Simpson," Dave said.

Murphy frowned, trying to recall the name. "Who the hell is that?" he said.

"An assistant district attorney from Penn, came in March of last year. Long brown hair, a little heavy, always wore slacks?"

Murphy's memory cleared as he recalled the Simpson woman. "Is she still here?"

Clendon shook his head. "She left to go into practice a couple of months ago."

"Why would she do it?" Murphy asked, listening eagerly but needing to get the facts straight.

Dave sighed. "It's a long story."

"I've got time."

"Well, I don't know if you remember, but Chloe was very ambitious. She pushed to get assigned to assist on the Harker case, thinking she could make a name with it. She interviewed the witness who gave her the information that would have exonerated Harker. She suppressed it because she wanted to have a conviction and get your attention that way, maybe win a promotion."

"She fixed the case, *too?*" Murphy asked in astonishment. He had hardly noticed the Simpson woman, never thought her capable of such deception, or much of anything else. She was clearly a drone, not a queen bee.

Dave nodded. "She fixed the case, all right, and then when you didn't pay attention to her, anyway, she got pissed off and gave the story to the newspapers after she left work here. Anonymously, of course."

"How do you know all this?"

Dave shifted his feet and didn't answer.

"You'd better tell me."

Dave sighed. "I was helping her pack up when she left and I saw the Harker file on her desk. I just picked it up out of curiosity and saw some notes and phone numbers written on the back cover. If you knew the background, and knew Chloe herself and the way her mind worked, it wasn't difficult to figure it out. She was convinced she was going to become a star here, and when that didn't happen, she took it personally and developed a real grudge against you."

"Why didn't you tell me this before?" Murphy asked. "For God's sake, man, I've been roasted alive in every rag in the state. You could at least have said that Simpson planned it herself and I had nothing to do with it. I might look like a bad manager who couldn't control his staff, but at least my integrity wouldn't have been questioned."

Dave closed his eyes, then opened them. "I know how strict your rules are about respecting the confidentiality of other people's cases. I thought you might fire me if you knew I had read Chloe's file. But as this thing went on and on, I couldn't stand to see you getting raked over the coals for it. So here I am."

"Fire you? Man, I just might kiss you!" Murphy leapt up and pounded Dave on the back, then pulled him out of his chair and hustled him toward the door.

"Sorry to be so abrupt, but I have a lot of phone calls to make. And then I have to figure out the best way to make a big apology to someone," Murphy said.

"Hope Jarvis?" Dave said from the doorway.

Murphy stared at him. "How did you know?"

"Boss, everybody knows. Everybody who has two eyes and a brain. That's another reason I finally came to you with this. The trouble between you two began about the time this story broke, and it occurred to me that the two events might be connected."

"Dave, you're a smart kid, and I'm sure you'll go far. Now get the hell out of here so I can begin to clean up this mess."

Dave grinned, saluted and left.

Murphy sat back in his chair, his mind racing. He knew his priority should be trying to extricate himself and his career from this debacle, but all he could think about was getting to Hope. Even though he now had proof of what he had felt in his heart—her innocence—he knew that would have no impact on his reception from her. He had rejected her, and she would still be furious about that.

But he had to try.

He stood up and headed for the door.

Hope was reclining by the pool, half-asleep after the traditional barbecue, when Meg's sister Pam came padding across the cement walkway and shook her shoulder.

Hope pushed back her sunglasses and sat up groggily. "What?" she said, looking around dazedly.

"Hope, there's somebody here to see you. Somebody from Philadelphia."

"Philadelphia?" Hope repeated stupidly.

"Yes. Dennis Murphy. He says he flew in today to see you. Meg is talking to him right now in the den."

"Dennis is here?" Hope said in alarm, standing up so suddenly that her beach jacket fell off her lap. She snatched it up and put it on over her bathing suit, belting it around her waist. She smoothed her damp hair behind her ears, remembered that she was wearing no makeup and sporting a new sunburn, and wanted to jump into the pool and drown herself.

"Don't you think you'd better see him?" Pam asked gently.

Hope nodded, stepped into her sandals and followed Pam through the sliding glass doors into the coolness of the house and then down the hall into the den. Murphy and Meg were sitting on a plaid divan, facing each other. Murphy stood when he saw Hope, the ice in his drink clinking with the motion.

"I think this is our cue to exit," Meg said to Pam, and the sisters filed out of the room quietly.

"What are you doing here?" Hope said to Murphy, as soon as they were gone.

"I wanted to apologize about the Harker case."

"The interstate telephone system isn't working?"

"I wanted to do it in person."

"How did you know where I was?"

"I got it out of the neighbor you asked to water your plants while you were away."

"I see." Hope looked at him, the jeans and loafers, the blue-striped cambric shirt she had never seen. He looked fabulous, damn him. She, on the other hand, looked like an overdone French fry in a towel robe.

"So what happened?" she asked sarcastically. "You had a divine revelation that I was telling the truth?"

"Dave Clendon knew who was responsible all along. He finally told me last night."

"How nice. It appears you have more faith in Dave Clendon than you have in me."

"I already knew you had done nothing wrong, Hope," Murphy said quietly. "I reached that conclusion as soon as I had time to calm down and think about it rationally."

"But you decided not to share that information with me?"

"I was afraid to call you."

"Then why are you here?" Hope asked frostily.

He shrugged. "I knew I had to face you. The conversation with Dave was just the catalyst. I couldn't just let you go on thinking what you were thinking. I knew you were innocent and wanted to tell you."

"It didn't occur to you that you were traveling 2,500 miles to tell me something I already knew?"

He looked away from her and said in a low tone, "I see you're not going to make this easy for me."

"Should I?" Hope countered coldly.

"I guess not."

Hope folded her arms and surveyed him as if he were a specimen on a glass slide. "Well, you've delivered your message. You can go now." She turned to leave.

He bolted in front of her, splashing his drink, and blocked the door.

"What am I supposed to do now?" Hope said. "Climb out the window?"

"Hope, I love you very much and want to marry you. I understand that you want to continue with your present career and I won't ask you to give it up. I'm not happy that you'll be dealing with criminals every day, but if that's what you want I'll have to accept it."

"What an enlightened attitude. When did you acquire it, flying over Kansas on the way out here?"

"Look, can't you just listen to me, give me a few minutes to explain?" he said, putting his drink down and then jamming his hands in his pockets.

"The way you listened to me?" she countered.

"I guess I'm asking you to be more generous than I was."

"That wouldn't be difficult. Exactly what is it that you need to explain, anyway? That you're a jackass? That you put me through hell because you don't have an ounce of trust or faith or compassion in your entire body?"

"Well, among other things."

Hope sat on the divan. "I already know all that, so no explanation is necessary. If you go back out into the hall, I'm sure Pam can show you to the door."

He stood staring at the floor, his hands in his pockets. "No second chance for me, huh?" he said bitterly. "Your clients all get one, but I don't?"

"My clients don't break my heart," Hope replied shortly. "I can't have a relationship with a man who doesn't trust me. That's the bottom line."

"I trust you, Hope. I was just scared, and it made me behave irrationally. Haven't you ever been scared?"

"You didn't say you were scared. You said you thought I had ratted on you about the Harker case."

"You've never heard of transference?"

"Look," Hope said, standing and facing him wearily. "I just don't want to discuss it anymore. I'm tired. I had to wear sunglasses for three days after your brilliant performance that Sunday morning. I had cried so much that my eyes were almost swollen shut. I can't go through that again. I won't."

"You won't have to go through it again," Murphy replied quietly. "What else can I say, except that I'm sorry?"

"I believe that you're sorry. It doesn't help. I don't want to see you anymore, Dennis. You're just too much work."

The finality in her tone at last convinced him to retreat. She didn't even sound angry, just exhausted. He was horrified to discover that his eyes were filling with tears, and he turned quickly, so that she wouldn't see his reaction.

"I'll go, then," he said huskily.

Hope didn't reply.

"I love you, Hope. I always will," he said softly, as he opened the door.

"I'm sorry you came all this way for nothing," she said dully.

"It wasn't for nothing. I got to see you again." He went into the hall, and she heard his footsteps receding, his voice as he said goodbye to her friends.

A minute later Meg came into the room and sat next to Hope on the divan. "No go, huh?"

Hope shook her head.

"You turned him down?"

"I had to."

"Why?"

Hope looked at the other woman. "You saw me after my last encounter with him. How can you ask that?"

"He made a mistake. We all do."

"You don't understand, Meg."

"Obviously not."

"Why are you always sticking up for him?" Hope inquired in exasperation.

"Maybe because I wish a man like that were in love with me, traveling from Pennsylvania to Arizona on a holiday just to plead with me to take him back. You don't realize how lucky you are."

"I don't feel very lucky. I'm in love with a crazy man."

"So you're still in love with him?"

"Of course, Meg. Did you think I could turn it off so easily, like a faucet?"

"Then why did you send him away?" Meg asked, in a tone of exaggerated patience.

"Self-preservation. He's too volatile. He resisted getting involved with me for as long as he could—I'm sure you remember that—and then once he *was* involved, he seized upon the first excuse he found to get out of it. There's a battle going on inside him, Meg, and I can sense that it's not over yet. He wants me, but at the same time he doesn't want the risk that goes along with caring about me."

"Give him a break, Hope. His first wife was murdered. That would make most people think twice about taking that chance again."

Hope put her head back against the cushion of the sofa and closed her eyes. "I know that. I understand that. But if I give him a second chance, what happens to me when he pulls back the next time? Do I have a nervous breakdown?"

"Maybe there won't be a next time. It's possible he's learned his lesson."

"I'm not convinced. He was too...brutal, Meg. He tried too hard to drive me away."

"I guess he succeeded."

A tear slipped down Hope's cheek and she wiped it away purposefully with the back of her hand.

"I know people get over these things," she said, forcing a bravery she didn't feel. "It's just that at this moment, it really doesn't seem possible."

"Come on, kiddo," Meg said, extending her hand to Hope. "Let's go back out by the pool. Maybe the sun will make you feel better."

Hope doubted it, but she rose obediently and followed her friend through the door.

Murphy stared out the window of the plane as it taxied down the runway in Philadelphia. He had felt awful when Claire died, but in a way this was worse, because he had nobody to blame for it but himself.

On some level he had known that Hope was tough, but he had never experienced that toughness directly until she stood in her friend's house and firmly, unwaveringly, told him to take a hike. Of course he deserved it, but it had still come as a shock. He had expected her to be angry, had anticipated outrage and hostility, but not the wall she had erected around herself which he couldn't breach.

Putting up walls was usually his department.

Well, she had learned from a good teacher.

He ignored the voice of the stewardess instructing the passengers not to remove their seat belts and concentrated on formulating a plan to get Hope back.

He hadn't given up, not by a long shot. His departure from Arizona was merely a tactical withdrawal until he could return, renewed, to do battle another day.

The legal community was like any other professional group—insulated and gossipy. He would be able to keep track of Hope and find out what she was doing.

Sooner or later, an opportunity would present itself.

And he would be there to take advantage of it.

He unclipped his belt as soon as the light went off and stepped into the aisle, heading for the exit.

About two weeks later, Hope returned from a session with Greg Collins, in which they'd been reorganizing her private practice, to find her mother sitting in her living room.

Hope's first reaction was alarm. Her mother had always had a key to her daughter's apartment, but it took a national disaster to get Mrs. Jarvis to leave Long Island. Her last departure had been when her sister died in South Carolina.

"What's wrong?" Hope said, dumping her purse on a chair and advancing into the room.

"Not a thing. I just wanted to talk to you," Mrs. Jarvis replied.

This in itself was suspicious. Hope's mother spent half her life on the telephone, since she rarely went anywhere in person. If she thought it necessary to conduct a face-to-face conversation, something must be up, for sure.

"Mother, what is it? Are you ill?" Hope sat next to the middle-aged woman on the sofa and searched her face anxiously. Although her mother was unquestionably the biggest cross to bear in her life, Hope didn't want anything to happen to her.

"Of course not, dear. I'm fine. I just had a visit from a friend of yours and I felt I should discuss it with you."

"A friend of mine?"

"Dennis Murphy."

Hope stared at her in amazed silence, then looked away, her mind racing. Dennis had gone behind her back and driven four hours to see Mrs. Jarvis to plead his case? Why, that conniver. She had to admire his nerve, but still she smoldered inwardly. This tactic was dirty pool.

"I see you're not happy about it," her mother said.

"Certainly not, Mother. My relationship with Dennis has nothing to do with you. He shouldn't have drawn you into it."

"It has something to do with me if he's going to be my son-in-law," Mrs. Jarvis replied.

"What gave you that idea?"

"Dennis said he wants to marry you."

"Then he also told you that I've turned him down."

"Yes, and that's what I wish to discuss."

Hope sighed and studied her mother, the carefully coiffed and sprayed hair, the Sherry Surprise lipstick she'd been wearing since 1960, the Ivory Velvet face powder which dated from the same era. Hope could well imagine the impact of Murphy's physical presence and Irish charm on this sixtyish matron whose only excitement since her husband's death stemmed from daytime television and parish bingo.

"Mother, before you say anything further, I just want to remind you that the last time we talked about this person on the phone you were convinced he was an alcoholic."

"Don't be ridiculous!" Mrs. Jarvis said in an outraged tone. "Dennis took me to dinner at the Ocean

Club and all he drank through the whole meal was mineral water.''

"The Ocean Club?" Hope said, amused.

"Yes, it was lovely. I had pâté and braised shrimp with baby vegetables and *crème brûlée* for dessert. There was a fresh breeze from the water, and we had such a nice table on the veranda.''

Hope wondered how much the "nice table" at the most exclusive restaurant on Long Island had cost her erstwhile lover. He had certainly pulled out all the stops to impress her mother and win her to his cause. What an operator he was! But Hope felt a flash of sympathy for him when she realized that he had undoubtedly been regaled by the whole story of Anna Jarvis's life, including her bout with chronic fatigue syndrome and the caesarean section she endured when giving birth to Hope.

"And I take it the topic of conversation during this idyllic interlude was my foolishness in refusing to marry your host?" Hope said dryly.

"Well, yes.''

"Mother, you don't know what happened," Hope said patiently, trying not to lose her temper.

"Yes, I do. Dennis told me all about it.''

*I'm sure not all,* Hope thought, remembering their passionate episodes in bed, as well as the Robert Kirk affair. If he *had* told her mother about that, she was going to shoot him in the head.

"What did he say?''

"That he had lost his first wife to a mugging, and as a result he was overprotective with you, and that caused him to behave badly, so you broke up with him."

Hope noticed that he had couched this essentially true information in the terms most likely to appeal to an anxious mother. "There was more to it than that, I can assure you."

"I assume so, dear, but while I hesitate to interfere in your personal business..."

Hope suppressed a smile.

"...I do think you should give this young man another chance. He seems very much in love with you, and he went to a great deal of trouble to contact me and talk to me about it."

"Mother, don't you see that your coming to me about this was exactly the result he wanted? He's manipulating you to get me to do what he wants."

"I don't see the harm in your just talking to him," Mrs. Jarvis said stubbornly, ignoring her daughter's observation.

Hope looked at the ceiling. She could see where this was going. If she didn't see Murphy, her mother was going to haunt her about it until she was deaf.

"All right, Mother, I'll meet with him. But it isn't going to change anything."

"You never know," her mother said, smiling archly.

"Have you had dinner?" Hope said, rising and going toward the kitchen, anxious to change the subject.

"No."

"Are you hungry?"

"Well, I guess I wouldn't mind a little something."

Hope opened the refrigerator to see what she had to feed her mother, planning Murphy's demise as she did.

The next day, in her lunch hour, Hope stopped off at Murphy's office, where Dave Clendon told her that Murphy was at an arraignment that had run late in the criminal courts building. Hope walked over to the designated courtroom and slipped into the last row of benches, watching Murphy perform.

He was dressed in a charcoal-gray three-piece suit that made him look like an Arrow shirt ad, his luxuriant hair clipped short since she had last seen him, his face tan from some excursion she had not shared. The very sight of him made her pulse race and her throat grow tight. She began to wonder whether she should leave, but the thought of Murphy having another tête-à-tête with her mother made her determined to stay. She was going to resolve this once and for all.

He looked up and spotted her, momentarily losing his train of thought and then recovering. She listened to him waltz around an inflexible judge for ten more minutes and finally reach a compromise which would keep the defendant in jail but on a lesser bail. When the matter was resolved, the arrested man's relatives filed out of the courtroom and the judge and bailiff disappeared into chambers. Murphy loaded and closed his briefcase and then came down the center aisle toward her, his expression wary.

"The Ocean Club, Dennis? You should be ashamed of yourself."

He grinned. "It worked, didn't it? You haven't returned my calls for two weeks, and here you are, in person."

"Bamboozling my mother is not going to win you any points with me."

His smile faded. "I wasn't bamboozling her. I just told her how much I loved you and that you wouldn't talk to me."

"Batting your baby blues the whole time, no doubt. How did you even get into the Ocean Club? It's members only, isn't it?"

"The Suffolk County D.A. is a member. He got me a guest pass."

"Aren't you the clever boy? Mom was suitably impressed."

"But not you, huh?" he said, watching her face.

"I'm impressed with your determination. It doesn't change anything between us."

"That's not strictly true, Hope."

"What do you mean?"

"I ran into Greg Collins at the bar luncheon for Judge Smithers. He told me that he will be handling all the criminal cases at your firm, and that you will be doing the discrimination cases and those falling under federal civil-rights legislation."

Hope was silent.

"So you took my advice," he said.

"I'm not stupid, Dennis. I can see that Greg will be better suited to deal with the criminal element than I am. For one thing, he has a lot more experience in that area. I'm not giving up First Amendment work, just reaching a sensible compromise."

"Why couldn't you do it for me?"

"You told me to go into real estate!"

"I just wanted you to avoid the Robert Kirks of the world."

"You were *ordering* me to do that, Dennis. You were making it a condition of our relationship. Can't you see that makes a big difference?"

He sighed and looked away from her. "So still no soap, huh?"

"No, Dennis. And please leave my mother alone. Conning her is off-limits. Period."

"You're really trying to make me pay, aren't you?" he said quietly, still not meeting her eyes.

"I'm not trying to do anything, Dennis, except get you to stay out of my life."

"That may be what you're telling yourself, honey, but you're enjoying every second of your self-righteous anger. You could have sent me a note about this, or left a message, but you wanted to show up in person and let me *see* you, let you see how much I still wanted you, so that driving the knife in would be that much sweeter."

Hope was uncomfortably aware that there was an element of truth in what he was saying. She had also wanted to see *him,* but she wasn't going to tell him that.

"Just leave me alone, Dennis," Hope said, and she walked out of the courtroom.

* * *

Three weeks later, Hope was sitting in her office, doing billing slips for her files, when Greg Collins knocked on her door and entered, his hands in his pockets, his expression grim.

"What is it, Greg?" Hope asked, glancing up at him and then putting her pen down. She had known Greg since they had taken a bar review course together several years ago, and she had seen him look like this only once before, when his father died.

"Dennis Murphy is in Hanneman Hospital," he said bluntly.

Hope was frozen in place, her eyes on his face.

"What happened?" she whispered.

"Car accident."

"How bad?"

"I don't know. It just came over the wire at the precinct. I was down there on the Monroe case."

Hope stood and reached for her purse.

"Where do you think you're going?" Greg said sharply, stepping into her path.

"I'm going down to the hospital," Hope replied.

"What for? You've been running away from the guy for over a month—now you're going to show up at his bedside and tell him all is forgiven because he's in traction?" Greg said.

"If you didn't want me to go there, why did you tell me where he was?" Hope asked, trying to push past him. "This is none of your damn business, anyway."

"It is my business," Greg replied, taking hold of her shoulders. "It's my business because Murphy has been calling me every couple of days to see how you were doing, swearing me to secrecy about it, of course. He was also the one who suggested to me that I handle the criminal cases that came into the firm, adding that when I passed it on to you, I should make it sound like it was my idea.''

Hope stared at him, stunned.

''He's crazy about you, Hope, looking out for your welfare when you won't even talk to him. I can't imagine what he did to deserve the treatment you've been giving him.''

''You don't know what happened,'' Hope said defensively, trying not to cry.

''No, I don't, and I don't care. I had a long talk with myself on the way over here, debating whether or not I should tell you about Murphy's accident. Then I realized you'd hear about it anyway, sooner or later, so it might as well be from me. But you'd better not go to that hospital looking for absolution.''

''Oh, shut up, Greg. And get out of the way.''

''I will not. If you're going to the hospital, I'm driving you there myself. You look like you're going to faint.''

''Oh, all right. Let's go.''

They went down to Greg's car in the underground garage, and Hope stared out the window as they drove through city traffic to the hospital. She knew that Greg was right; she'd been enjoying torturing Murphy, been smug and satisfied with his contrition, and it had taken an event like this to make her see her foolishness for what it was. She only hoped that she would have the chance to make it up to him.

Greg was silent until they pulled into the parking lot, and then he said quietly, "Hope, nobody's more stubborn than you are when you think you're right. It's an asset in our practice, but in private life it can be hell. Whatever Murphy did, let it go. You wouldn't be here if you didn't love him, right?"

She nodded, reaching for the door handle.

"Greg, don't come in, all right? And would you call my friend Meg and ask her to meet me here? I think I'll need the moral support," Hope said.

Greg nodded, watching as she got out of the car and walked toward the hospital entrance. Then he backed out of the space and left the parking lot.

Hope entered the lobby and went to the information desk to find out where Murphy was. She took the elevator to his floor, a knot of nervousness in her stomach, her hands clenched tightly on the strap of her purse.

When the doors of the elevator opened, she was assaulted by the hospital smells of ether and disinfectant and body fluids, the pervasive miasma of illness. Swallowing hard, she walked past the nurse's station and followed the signs for the numbered rooms. She located Murphy's when she saw his brother, Hugh, standing outside of it, conferring with another doctor.

"Hello, Hugh," she said gingerly, when he looked up from his conversation.

"What are you doing here?" he replied, abandoning his companion and walking toward her. His expression was not welcoming.

"Hugh, I can only imagine what Dennis has been telling you about me, but you have to let me see him."

"Why? So you can feel better about the way you've been treating him?"

"Is he all right?" Hope asked, ignoring Hugh's response.

"He's got a broken leg, multiple contusions and abrasions, and a severe concussion. Right now he's asleep."

"Will he be okay?"

"He should be. We'll have the results of the CAT scan in a few hours."

"Can I sit with him until he wakes up?" Hope asked, sighing with relief.

"I don't want you upsetting him."

"I'm not going to upset him. I want to tell him I've been wrong and I'm willing to give it another try." She paused meaningfully. "I think he will be glad to hear that."

Hugh hesitated.

"Please, Hugh. I want to help."

He nodded finally and said, "I'll tell the nurse to let you stay."

Hope put her hand on his arm. "Thanks, Hugh."

"Go on in," he said, and turned away.

Hope went into the room, past the drawn curtain around the bed of Dennis's roommate, and stopped short when she saw Dennis ensconced in the neighboring bed. He was pale beneath his new tan, his head swathed in bandages, his left leg in a plaster cast poking out from under the sheet. She took the hand lying on top of the cotton blanket, but he didn't move.

Hope drew a chair up next to his bed and sat. She watched him, and dozed, and looked out the window. Several hours passed before she glanced back at his bed and saw that he was watching her.

"Hope?" he murmured.

"Yes, I'm right here," she said, squeezing his hand.

"Thought . . . was dreaming."

"No. I'm here. I'm back, Dennis. For good."

"For . . . good?"

"That's right. Now go back to sleep. I'll be here when you wake up.

"Promise?"

"I promise."

His eyes closed, and Hope used her free hand to wipe her streaming eyes.

Then she settled in to wait.

* * * * *

**Rugged and lean...and the best-looking,
sweetest-talking men to be found in the
entire Lone Star state!**

*Diana
Palmer*

LONG, TALL
TEXANS

In July 1994, Silhouette is very proud to bring you
Diana Palmer's first three LONG, TALL TEXANS.
CALHOUN, JUSTIN and TYLER—the three cowboys
who started the legend. Now they're back by popular
demand in one classic volume—and they're ready to
lasso your heart! Beautifully repackaged for this
special event, this collection is sure to be a
longtime keepsake!

"Diana Palmer makes a reader want to find a Texan
of her own to love!"
—*Affaire de Coeur*

**LONG, TALL TEXANS—the first three—
reunited in this special roundup!**

**Available in July,
wherever Silhouette books are sold.**

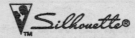

# Take 4 bestselling love stories FREE

## Plus get a FREE surprise gift!

## Special Limited-time Offer

**Mail to Silhouette Reader Service™**

3010 Walden Avenue
P.O. Box 1867
Buffalo, N.Y. 14269-1867

**YES!** Please send me 4 free Silhouette Desire® novels and my free surprise gift. Then send me 6 brand-new novels every month, which I will receive months before they appear in bookstores. Bill me at the low price of $2.44 each plus 25¢ delivery and applicable sales tax, if any.* That's the complete price and—compared to the cover prices of $2.99 each—quite a bargain! I understand that accepting the books and gift places me under no obligation ever to buy any books. I can always return a shipment and cancel at any time. Even if I never buy another book from Silhouette, the 4 free books and the surprise gift are mine to keep forever.

225 BPA ANRS

| | | |
|---|---|---|
| Name | (PLEASE PRINT) | |
| Address | | Apt. No. |
| City | State | Zip |

This offer is limited to one order per household and not valid to present Silhouette Desire® subscribers. *Terms and prices are subject to change without notice.
Sales tax applicable in N.Y.

UDES-94R

**Silhouette Books
is proud to present
our best authors, their best books...
and the best in your reading pleasure!**

**Throughout 1994, look for exciting books
by these top names in contemporary
romance:**

**DIANA PALMER**
*Enamored* in August

**HEATHER GRAHAM POZZESSERE**
*The Game of Love* in August

**FERN MICHAELS**
*Beyond Tomorrow* in August

**NORA ROBERTS**
*The Last Honest Woman* in September

**LINDA LAEL MILLER**
*Snowflakes on the Sea* in September

*When it comes to passion,
we wrote the book.*

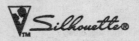

Fifty red-blooded, white-hot, true-blue hunks
from every State in the Union!

Look for MEN MADE IN AMERICA! Written by some of
our most popular authors, these stories feature fifty of the
strongest, sexiest men, each from a different state in the
union!

Two titles available every month at your favorite retail
outlet.

In July, look for:

ROCKY ROAD by Anne Stuart (Maine)
THE LOVE THING by Dixie Browning (Maryland)

In August, look for:

PROS AND CONS by Bethany Campbell (Massachusetts)
TO TAME A WOLF by Anne McAllister (Michigan)

**You won't be able to resist MEN MADE IN AMERICA!**

# SILHOUETTE®
## *Desire*®

**They're sexy, they're determined, they're trouble
with a capital *T*!**

Meet six of the steamiest, most stubborn heroes you'd ever
want to know, and learn *everything* about them....

August's *Man of the Month,* Quinn Donovan, in
**FUSION** by Cait London

**Mr. Bad Timing,** Dan Kingman, in
**DREAMS AND SCHEMES** by Merline Lovelace

**Mr. Marriage-phobic,** Connor Devlin, in
**WHAT ARE FRIENDS FOR?** by Naomi Horton

**Mr. Sensible,** Lucas McCall, in **HOT PROPERTY**
by Rita Rainville

**Mr. Know-it-all,** Thomas Kane, in **NIGHTFIRE**
by Barbara McCauley

**Mr. Macho,** Jake Powers, in **LOVE POWER**
by Susan Carroll

Look for them on the covers so you can see just how
handsome and irresistible they are!

**Coming in August only from Silhouette Desire!**    CENTER